Object Coach

Tom Lee

Tom Lee is a writer known for his interest in landscape, technology and the senses. He grew up on a farm near Orange in Central-West NSW, and is a senior lecturer in the Faculty of Design, Architecture and Building at the University of Technology Sydney. Tom was named a *Sydney Morning Herald* Best Young Australian Novelist in 2019 and his first novel, *Coach Fitz*, was longlisted for the Voss Literary Prize in the same year.

Tom Lee

Object Coach

A Novel

First published in Australia in 2022
by Upswell Publishing
Perth, Western Australia
upswellpublishing.com

ISBN: 978-0-6452480-6-7

A catalogue record for this
book is available from the
National Library of Australia

NATIONAL
LIBRARY
OF AUSTRALIA

Cover design by Chil3, Fremantle
Typeset in Foundry Origin by Lasertype
Printed by McPherson's Printing Group

9. Destiny

Beta had invited me to be a respondent at a seminar where the internationally recognised scholar was giving a talk. Her most recent research combined a philosophical interpretation of the discipline design with fiction writing. The scholar, let's call her Destiny, had shared a document before the event outlining the theoretical principles and fictional exemplars relevant to her yet-to-be-completed project based on this research. This document would form the basis of my response.

Destiny's project closely resembled my own. I wrote in my email response to Beta that I found the affinities spooky.

As I read through the document, however, I began to form more nuanced ideas about how our two projects corresponded and differed. It was like the event of seeing a familiar face in a crowd resolve into that of a stranger on closer inspection. A stranger with their own autonomous, parallel trajectory, but familiar-looking nonetheless.

I jotted down my notes in a TextEdit window on my laptop that I flicked between while I read the PDF Destiny had shared. While Destiny's talk was not intended to be a comprehensive account of her project, it did give me a clear indication of some of the areas I might speak towards in order to make the event valuable for the audience and perhaps even for Destiny.

It had become customary for me to speak my ideas for any sort of public talk out loud into an audio recording device, often while lying down on the grass under two large fig trees, in a park not far from the campus where I worked. Something about lying down and looking up at the trees made it easier to articulate my thoughts, as though the branches were a visual analogue for the sentences I was attempting to speak. Lying down also seemed to reduce some of the exasperation I felt when trying to communicate complex ideas to other humans face-to-face. Many of my colleagues complained about communicating through email and video calls, however, upright, frontally oriented communication was, in my experience, equally inhibiting to the lucid and enjoyable exchanges that were part of the substance of life.

I would run my hands through the grass as though I were playing with the hair of some divine being, reclining back with one arm tucked behind my head, as I continued to speak upwards into the air, in what I imagined was a plume of smoke.

I simply pressed record on my smartphone, using an app that sat alongside Compass, Contacts, Find My Phone and the somewhat perplexing Tips, which I had never thought to explore.

I pressed record.

The first thing I would like to say to Destiny, I said, is that I too am interested in using narrative to explore the relationship between the imagination and technology. Among the things that motivate me most in this regard is giving voice or character to the artificial. I have an impression of beings to whom I must give voice. These are not human beings as such, but the shifting technological forms through which humans act, whether personally or as a collective. Not the androids and cyborgs and aliens of science fiction, but the unremarkable, omnipresent forms used to wrest the world to our minor advantage. The dream machines of vernacular life.

Take the backpack, for example, with its numerous compartments, its distinct look and connotations, the perhaps unsettling, grubby feeling of grains accumulated in certain of its pockets, and the routines that weave that backpack into the different trajectories taken through life; the situation of the backpack in relation to a broader set of devices that might be transported within it, and the different though comparable spaces of personal storage like lockers, pockets and handbags; how the backpack might either acquire new meaning with time, whether in a positive sense to become cherished, or negative, as something irritating or maybe even the sign of a certain embarrassment; and lastly, how the backpack came to be made from particular materials, where and how these were sourced, and the processes of transformation and movement that brought these materials and agents of production together in a particular form.

Science fiction tends to be the imaginative playground where artificial beings were given voice. Important precedents and conventions of the genre have, however, led to a seeming obsession with technological innovation and the extreme, often dystopian, world-changing potentials that might flow from powerful new technologies, rendered in isolation from the ordinary aspects of everyday life. Science fiction narratives typically possesses two key features in this sense: a storyworld or setting that departed in a pronounced way from the known possibilities of the real or the empirical—places like islands, space stations and other planets being the prime examples—and the presence of unfamiliar, world-shaping novelties, technological innovations like time machines and robots, or alien beings with special abilities. Consequently, science fiction often requires a significant amount of exposition, leaving far less time to spend on other things, whatever they might be, perhaps the inherently fictive or surreal qualities of selfhood or place, for example.

My attention drifted from the demands of my recording device and the imagined audience that required a systematic presentation of my ideas. I looked up at the branches of the two figs extending above me, and I conceived myself as floating in a womb-like space, elevated on a soft grass platform, with my mind plugged in to this idealised interface, where my conscious experience, my senses, memories and emotions, blended seamlessly into the surrounding environment.

I now spoke silently to myself; that disordered, reflective, sometimes barely conscious manner of speaking, which in a sense could be considered the substance of my inner life.

While Destiny and I might have shared similar sentiments regarding the subject matter of our respective research interest, she had, however, cited the works of a certain novelist in her document as an exemplar that exhibited a very different sensibility to the authors I liked. Destiny didn't go into any detail in her introductory document about how the fiction of this named exemplar was considered in her own broader writing project; whether the author's work had been selected based on the content of the narratives, the structures of the plot, the style or the tone of the writing, the use of character, or some other difficult-to-identify feature of the works. But the name sat there like a blemish and the less generous aspect of my attitude fought to dismiss the value of her project outright.

In the absence of an explanation, I wondered how my own crop of authors had or might come to influence my fiction writing project. There were three authors whose books I felt I had inhabited for enough time for the tone and content of their works to become like something akin to an acquired cognitive modality, not unlike the voice of a parent or close friend that possesses a seemingly autonomous, internally experienced agency over our thoughts. Each author had been lauded by contemporary literary critics for several reasons: innovativeness when it came to reinterpreting the conventions of form; distinctive and coherent literary voice; and for demonstrated expertise in constructing sentences and sets of sentences.

I had been advised by the scholarly community where I spent most of my time that the fictions I wrote and spoke within our institution— fictions that were in part inspired by the aforementioned authors to whom I still in some senses saw myself apprenticed—demonstrated an overlap between the mental act of designing and a certain literary or poetic sensibility. My colleagues had suggested that modern literature might be improved if writers understood design better, and could give more interested and reflective accounts of the often-inconspicuous images, spaces and things that arrived in our world, sometimes seemingly without purpose or meaning. In their more generous moments, my colleagues had interpreted my writing as a new genre or subgenre that explored the emotional and mental states experienced during the acts of designing, thereby giving designers a language to better communicate their design practices and habits.

I stood up to address the park as though it were a packed auditorium and I was delivering some concluding considerations in my response to Destiny's document.

Perhaps shaken free by my upright posture, my thoughts escaped me at this point, scattered like loose change on the ground. Instead my mind filled with the landscape: the distant patch of cold blue sky that became visible, briefly, to the north before disappearing again behind the bright, brown-grey clouds; the sharply angled, mantis-like streetlights that lit the paths through the park, and the games of basketball persisting despite the beginnings of light rain; the evening squawk of the bats and the birds in the trees; an odd-shaped figure with long, dangly arms, as though they had been stretched out on a rack; the things I'd seen, in a sense, or rather felt, but which were not exactly visible in my present perceptual field: the vanished impressions of peoples' movements; the ghost forms of the figures from further back in the past, who once played tennis on the overgrown ground where I sat, figures dressed in white, hitting balls back and forth, their laughter and the pleasing thwack of the balls against racquets mixing with games of the presently observed players on the newer courts nearby.

I lay back down in the grass, closed my eyes, and attempted to reconstruct the scene I had just witnessed in the darkness of my mind.

***

Beta organised a dinner at a nearby restaurant after the event with Destiny. There were only five of us, including myself: Destiny, Beta, another senior colleague, Tobe, and Marta, a previous research student who now worked in the design industry.

The restaurant space was beautifully designed. There was an open kitchen in the centre, showing the chefs at work in their white uniforms. The tables and chairs were made of blonde timber and the walls and floor were cement. The drinks menu was encased in a soft leather folder and the waitstaff appeared with the unobtrusive regularity that is the mark of professionalism in the industry, asking after our dietary requirements and preferences in wine.

We all clustered around one end of the table and became distracted in talk. I had the impression, initially, that Destiny was uncomfortable in this environment. I suspected my read of the situation may have been influenced by certain assumptions I'd made about her character, such as an austerity and principled resistance to spaces of consumption, of which this was a prime example. She seemed bothered by the waitstaff who came to ask about our drinks and she made little effort to engage anyone else on the table in conversation, despite being the focal point of our gathering.

The group, led by Marta, came to the decision that we would choose a bottle of wine. This first decision entailed a further one: what kind of wine would we get? Destiny was not interested in the discussion. She waved the questions away and continued to slump in her chair. Destiny did not drink alcohol. Tobe said he would leave the decision up to the rest of us, not because he didn't want to drink any wine, but to make the process easier since he didn't know that much about it. Tobe had recently started taking an interest in beer. Marta suggested we choose a light red, on account of the versatility of this type of wine as an accompaniment for the dishes on the menu we were likely to choose. Beta and I agreed this sounded like a good idea.

Light red entailed another decision: which kind of light red? Marta said she liked reds with the flavour of berries.

I'm the opposite, I said. I like minerally reds.

That's OK, said Marta.

I like berry too, said Beta.

Do you know much about wines, Tom?, asked Tobe.

I know a few words, I said, one of which is *minerally*. For some reason, this word has come to represent a particularly prized quality.

Is it like 'flinty'? asked Toby

Yes, yes, I said. Also, 'chalky'. Though saying this, I am not so sure.

In attempting to specify this exact quality, I continued, I think of clear water running through steep limestone gorges, and of the water that pools in oyster shells. I think of an elixir that is at once perfectly adapted to my body and yet not of my body, in the sense that I imagine my liquid essence to be sweet, fatty and acidic, simply on account of the foods I consume. As a consequence, I have come to associate the strong scent of berries and other floral aromas in wine with the absence of this sought after but vaguely defined minerally quality, which is the first thing I mention to people in bottle shops and restaurants who I imagine as experts.

I hate wine snobs, Destiny said to me with a smirk, as though we were both in on a joke.

When I was on a flight back from Greece last year, began Marta, unperturbed by Destiny's interjection—when I was flying back from Greece, one of the ordinary and yet reliably pleasing things I thought about was a bottle of wine packed in among the clothes in my suitcase. I'd bought the wine in Lefkada, on my second last day in the country. Less than a litre of fermented grape juice in a glass bottle, said Marta, that I planned to drink in quarantine over two or three nights when I returned. I thought to myself: I will drink the wine and then it will be gone. I'll put the bottle in the recycling bin and it will be gone too. There'll be no trace of its substance in my life. But on that flight, the thought of that wine made me happy; it was a transparent green-yellow potion, suspended in its protective glass bottle among my clothes while we hurtled across the globe, and thinking about it made me happy enough to suppress the sense of disappointment I then felt about the many cancelled plans for socialising; happy enough to ignore the challenges of the rest of the flight; happy enough to give me a sense of fortitude in a world that had started to appear increasingly unsteady. And the beauty of it is, said Marta, that the comparatively trivial nature of the treasure seemed to magnify its powers.

When the waiter next came we gave him our order, which included a bottle of light red wine with berry-like qualities.

What makes me happy, responded Beta, is our shack in the mountains. It's only small, but one of the greatest sources of anxiety for me about this virus is the sense that in the city I'm more exposed to it. As things got worse, I started to think more and more of our little yard and the sense of security that came from feeling confidently unobserved. It made me feel warm. It's not something I usually feel, at least not to this extent. I suppose it's because I feel safe there. Perhaps your wine is like this, gave you something like this feeling?

The lights in the restaurant dimmed further and I noticed Destiny had started to become anxious. She was grasping the edge of the table and was looking about skittishly. She interrupted Beta with a whisper, who repeated what she said at higher volume: Your heart's racing? A tablet? You alright?

Destiny gave Beta an irritated shush and they continued to talk at a whisper.

I started to worry about Destiny and the source of her anxiety: was it concern about the virus in this a busy, enclosed space? Or had something else in the environment spooked her?

Might I, in fact, be the source of her anxiety? Could her apprehension have been caused by something I said in my seminar response earlier that day? Or was it because I bought my own cushion to sit on, due to the hard seats that were common in restaurants and which irritated a nerve issue in my upper hamstring? Was it the inane talk about wine, the sheer number of decisions that needed to be made about inconsequential things? Was it the waitstaff, appearing silently from the shadows to refill our glasses and make enquires as to whether we were OK?

The talk returned to wine. While Tobe had some misgivings about all the fuss people made about it, he reasoned that there were far worse things people could be doing with their time. There was, Tobe thought, something redeeming about people delighting in and placing value on hedonistic phenomena.

I have always liked the idea, said Tobe, that we train ourselves to become more sensitive and wise by the subtle distinctions we give to various substances, forms and materials. It's tempting to be cynical about this, but our capacity to make what might seem like frivolous distinctions is also a reflection of our capacity to enlarge our appetites for concern.

What about shotguns? mumbled Destiny—offering what I guessed she thought was a counter example to Tobe's proposition.

Tobe and the others didn't hear, but I did, and Destiny saw my recognition and leant in towards me.

There are communities of shotgun aficionados, she said, as though this comment in itself summed things up.

Marta was, as far as I could tell, now talking about an image of some sort—I had missed the first part of the conversation.

The uniform, softly luminous leather and the frayed chaos of the coloured cotton seared an impression in my mind, said Marta.

When our meals arrived, one of the waitstaff presented them with a faultless and authoritative description of the different ingredients and techniques for preparation. She gave a subdued bow at the conclusion of her speech and then rejoined the flow of activity between the different tables and the kitchen.

Now the food was on the table, Destiny seemed to relax. She asked who was going to be brave enough to cut a large, charred cabbage into portions. I took up the offer and drew attention to the woman who had presented our meals.

That was impressive, I said, while struggling to cut through the cabbage with a spoon.

I know, said Marta, who then confessed she had been thinking recently of organising a training event for her workplace that involved the best-of-the-best in the hospitality industry sharing their insights about food service in restaurants, cafes and bars for the purpose of improving the design of digital services, which relied largely on screen-based interfaces.

In her internet research, Marta had become fixated on the general manager of a certain restaurant who had recently won a prestigious award.

I would imagine her welcoming guests with warmth into her restaurant, said Marta, inviting them into her sense of confidence with a kind of conservation that trod the fine line between conviviality and distance, and left everyone reassured their obscure tastes would be matched exactly with whatever food and drink they wished to consume.

Marta discovered the general manager in question was also an amateur boxer. She tried to find details about the gym where the manager boxed. The closest she got was a story in *Gourmet Food* magazine that featured a black-and-white image of the manager standing next to a shiny rack of medicine balls and wearing an open sports jacket with metallic, silver lining.

I can still recall the details of image, said Marta. She had one arm resting on the rack, with one hand just out of the shot. Her other hand was in the pocket of her designer boxer shorts. Something about the quality of the image made it look as though her eyes were made from the same metallic substance as the jacket.

The idea that the manager was a consummate professional, trained in the techniques of the hospitality industry, and the knowledge that she was an athlete of some ability, left Marta burdened with the fantasy that she might build an entire business idea around the service experience created by the manager, even to the extent that she imagined a digital assistant modelled on her look and attitude.

Though I soon began to wonder, said Marta, whether my initial visions of such a technology looking and acting like the manager were significantly misguided. For the skill in that role, as in many service roles, lies in a hyper-attentiveness to gestural cues, particularly those associated with the face and the eyes.

Marta said that doing justice to the inspiration she obtained from professionals working the floor in the hospitality industry would require training her hypothetical digital assistant to appear exactly when, and only when, people needed it.

And if the perceptiveness of a highly qualified human was replicated for such ends, then what, wondered Marta, were the implications? Both for the people who currently relied on exercising such aptitudes for their employment, and those who might turn the technology to other, less agreeable ends, as they surely would?

Another waiter bought the final plate of food and placed it on the table, announcing its contents to the group.

He's not as good, said Marta, picking up her cutlery in a way that made me regard her as mischievous.

Beta asked Destiny whether she wanted any of the lamb dish we had ordered and with some irritation she said no, she didn't eat red meat anymore, not since her illness.

Destiny clearly didn't want to talk any further on the matter but Marta and Beta in their friendly, inquisitive manner, asked her to elaborate. I chimed in too, since questions of personal taste were among my favoured topics of conversation.

Destiny revealed she had recently been beset by an illness of a kind she had not previously experienced.

Though to call it an illness is a bit misleading, she said, now seeming to settle into the stage we'd readied for her to tell the story. She mumbled, barely moving her lips, and her face dipped in and out of a spot of light as she talked, which gave certain moments in the story emphasis. I detected what I thought was a submerged Dutch accent, or perhaps South African.

Whenever Destiny had listed her symptoms to those who cared to listen, they regarded her with disbelief: *it doesn't sound like you're sick to me, it sounds like you're getting older*, one friend advised. Nonetheless, as arguments to the contrary mounted, she remained convinced that the suddenness of these changes in her constitution could only mean that she was sick, which is to say, she'd caught something, her immune system breached by some variety of pathogen.

Destiny was not the kind of person who usually placed much emphasis on how she felt and had indeed been proud, to some degree, of not placing demands on other people regarding her needs, preferences and the vagaries of her imagination. She referred to our table being asked whether we had any allergens only moments ago, and admitted that when no one mentioned any, she felt a mild sense of shame and decided, as she often did, not to draw attention to those foods that seemed not to agree with her. Ordering food in group contexts entailed an onslaught of disagreeable, distracting emotions with which she'd rather not keep company.

The symptoms of her illness included a light pain behind the eyes and tiredness throughout the day. This tiredness was most severe in the mornings and evenings (usually an early riser Destiny now found herself sleeping in). She was increasingly prone to dizzy spells when she stood up, and a host of old injuries—a sore ankle, a broken finger, a ruptured disk in her back—again resonated with a dull pain. She also experienced a change in her appetite.

I don't care to go through them all for you now, said Destiny, but red meat and alcohol no longer offer much appeal.

Perhaps you are pregnant? offered Marta.

To my surprise, Destiny smirked sportingly and continued her account.

She felt that she could, after a fashion, manipulate the presence of the illness by acting a certain way and performing certain activities, although she could never banish the feeling entirely. Increasingly she didn't feel like exercising, however when she did exercise, it would feel for a while like she was no longer ill, at least not to the same degree. This characterised her energy levels more generally; it wasn't that she lacked the energy as such but she lacked the initial capacity to motivate herself to become energised. Destiny knew to some extent what might do her good, but no longer found it imperative.

According to Destiny, her most unusual symptom related to her hearing. She found herself increasingly sensitive to certain frequencies, of which her partner was entirely unaware. She had started hearing a humming sound in the pipes, channels and electrics that knitted her apartment into the larger, comfort-sustaining infrastructure of the building and city. She'd never noticed this sound before but now it composed the texture of her experience, and her partner's inability to sense the sound felt like a denial of the agreed-upon reality they once shared. Destiny knew, at a rational level, that she couldn't expect her partner to hear what she simply couldn't hear. But this didn't seem to ameliorate the growing feeling of alienation she now felt creeping into the relationship.

In all seriousness, said Destiny, I wonder how many bonds disintegrate on account of different perceptual tunings. I fear our relationship is in its final phase.

Destiny said she found some solace in the fantasy that every virus was in fact a technology designed by a civilisation of beings invisible to humans, and that humans in turn were the creators of viruses that invaded other civilisations for whom we were invisible.

I switch between this fantasy, and the more solemn idea that in some sense my existence now testifies to the presence of my illness, said Destiny, and that I have the duty of slowly removing myself from public life in order to sing the praises and sorrows of this new appetite I seem to have acquired.

A long silence passed over the table. The plates of food with the final remains of our meals were shuffled among the group, before the wait-staff appeared once again and whisked them away. New conversations about people whose names I didn't know started up between Tobe, Beta and Marta.

Destiny, observing my inability to enter into the discussion, mumbled something in my direction and I lent in more closely to hear her repeat it.

I wanted to talk to you, she said.

At first I thought she meant now, outside, however Destiny then asked whether I would like to accompany her the next morning to an exhibition that was showing at a museum near the university. I sensed she wished to convey that this invitation was a gesture of profound importance and I couldn't help but be taken up by the notion, fanciful though it was, that I had been chosen by Destiny as *the one* among our table, that I had passed the test which had been set and would now come to enjoy the fruits of my intellectual and creative labours.

We exited the restaurant not long after and said our goodbyes on the street in the cool night air. Destiny, much to my surprise, placed a baseball cap on her head, which seemed at once entirely incongruous and yet a perfect finishing touch. She was smaller than she'd seemed both at the table during dinner and at the talk earlier that day, as though the exterior environment, or lack of an interior, impacted her relative scale in a different manner to my other companions. I wondered whether she'd announce our appointment tomorrow or if any of the others even knew of the arrangement.

Nine o'clock, she said, when we shook hands, and then turned to walk with Beta back towards the university. Marta, Tobe and I walked for a short while together in the other direction; soon Tobe peeled off, then Marta, and I was alone; that peculiar kind of secure aloneness that comes in the wake of convivial social encounters where we find ourselves confirmed as beings of some value on account of being recognised by our peers.

***

On my way to the museum I'd become emotional listening to a song on my smartphone and had to brush the tears from my face as I approached Destiny, who was waiting by the concierge with her cap in her hand. I hoped she'd assume my tears were the result of the cold air.

We put our bags and jackets in a locker, still operated, somewhat endearingly, by a small round token obtained from the concierge. The first exhibit was a display of weapons and armour collected from across the globe, on loan from a sister institution in the northern hemisphere.

I immediately noticed a certain energy in Destiny, a bounce in her step that was absent the previous night. It seemed to me that the displays in the museum allowed her to move freely among her interests, whereas last night she had been constrained by the rituals of restaurant dining and was perhaps exhausted by the talk earlier that day.

We paused at a series of glass display boxes that contained several impressive handguns and rifles from 16th-century Germany with carved ivory inlays depicting scenes of the hunt. Destiny asked why I thought it was so important for these weapons to appear beautiful when their purpose was for killing. Were they not simply functional tools?

I reflected on this question for a while, suspecting it was the gateway to some further discourse on the relationship between humans, tools and aesthetics, and eventually suggested that the weapons were no doubt also items of status, used to indicate the power and privilege of their owners.

Do they become better fighters as a consequence of these inscribed reminders of power and identity, asked Destiny?

Some things do make us feel differently, I said halfheartedly.

I assume you know the story of Balfour and her stick, said Destiny?

When I said that I did not know the story, Destiny circled around to the other side of the cabinet so that we stood on opposite sides and she spoke towards the glass that separated our standpoints as though the story she told emerged from the surface, occasionally gesturing with an open hand to indicate moments of portents or ambiguity.

Apparently Balfour was a renowned competitor at sport known as Dundupple, a popular tradition among a large network of families that crisscrossed the border between England and Scotland. She had for many generations been unbeatable in the annual Dundupple festivals held by the various families in succession during the summer. One year, however, when Balfour was arguably in her prime as a competitor, she misplaced her Dundupple stick. Some in the family suspected it was stolen. Balfour's stick, like the sticks of Dundupple players from all the participating families, was inscribed with markings from over the generations that represented certain events of significance both directly and indirectly related to the festivals—certain seasonal peculiarities, idiomatic jokes, caricatures of particular local characters, and visualisations of the results intended to highlight certain relationships in the competition data that weren't obvious in the format used in historical records. Balfour was faced with the choice of either using her comparatively plain backup stick or borrowing the stick of another member of her family. She first tried using her backup stick and soon found that even the shots she had been able to execute with ease previously, now became significant trials of coordination. At the next festival Balfour then tried the stick of another family member in desperation only to find that her performance got worse still and soon the members of other competing families were busily inscribing symbols and images into their sticks that told of the transformation of Balfour from virtuoso to fool. Indeed, even members of her own family were compelled to focus on that aspect of the festivals in their inscriptions on account of its undeniable significance when compared to other events that year. In the time between penultimate and the last Dundupple festival, Balfour sought out the help of Gary, a mysterious figure who had been recommended to her by a cousin. Gary had moved back to the region recently and tried to claim blood linage with Balfour's family only for them to reject his advances, whether on account of the untruthfulness of his claims or a certain disagreeable aspect of his character it was hard to tell. Balfour's cousin, however, had had the chance to see inside Gary's home and saw that he seemed to spend all the time he was forced to spend alone creating intricately inscribed Dundupple sticks that were useless in themselves, and told stories of an entirely self-referential nature, though which demonstrated his ability to render complex emotional and psychological events onto a hard, curved surface of limited dimensions—such was the nature of all Dundupple sticks. So Balfour went to visit Gary with her backup stick and there she sat in the relative darkness of his living room where he plied her with his homemade fermentations and busily inscribed the stories she soon felt compelled to elaborate in the atmospheric setting of his house and under the influence of his strange beverages. Balfour's sittings took place over many days and when she finally emerged from

Gary's house with her new stick and showed it to the other, more respected members of her family, they saw that it depicted events of an altogether different nature to the events they were accustomed to seeing on Dundupple sticks.

At the last Dundupple festival for that year Balfour started very nervously with her new stick, playing only marginally better than she had with the previous stick she had borrowed from a family member. Then at the point when it had almost become impossible for her to recover from her until that point mediocre performance, something in Balfour changed. She looked upon her stick in the unrelenting late summer light, pulled a knife from her pocket and made what appeared to be some further, initial augmentations of Gary's designs which she then finished in the shade of a nearby oak while the other players completed the round.

When Balfour next stood to compete she exuded an air of confidence and calmness that reminded everyone of the player she had once been and her following efforts testified to the truth of what they saw in her changed comportment. Against all odds Balfour managed to secure a victory. Her action, while stable and strong as before had now acquired a new dimension, something perhaps even vaguely out of control or shambolic. The half-finished stories on the sticks of family members were supplemented to tell both of Balfour and her new stick and of Gary, his abilities, his strange home and his drinks.

Balfour went to visit and thank Gary immediately after the festival celebrations. She was hoping he would join some of the post-festival activities and was planning to invite him to the Dundupple competition next year. When Balfour arrived at Gary's house, however, it had been largely cleared of his possessions, aside from a few of the bigger empty vats that he used for his fermentations and the scattered remnants of his stick-inscribing efforts. As Balfour spent some more time in that space and her perception opened to the fine distinction between things that have been haphazardly and deliberately arranged, she noticed one unusual looking stick leaning against the wall. The stick was free from inscriptions and the wood looked soft and impressionable, so soft, in fact, that when Balfour took it in her hands it seemed to mould to her grip and even the lightest touch of her fingers. Unsure of what to do with the stick, in a moment of heated uncertainty, Balfour broke it over her knee and threw it against the wall before hurrying from the house and out into the fields beyond where she soon rejoined her family and extended family in celebrations of merriment and contemplation.

At this point Destiny paused for a while, then looked over to me in a gesture that signaled she wanted to move on to the next room. As we walked, she continued the story.

Balfour never won another Dundupple festival. She competed the next year and the next year after that, and then stopped competing altogether. Her stick, the one made by Gary, subsequently became the trophy for the event after she passed away and to my knowledge it remains the trophy used by the families today.

Destiny and I gradually drifted apart as we entered the next room, which was far larger and filled with ceramics in glass cabinets. I inspected the items behind the glass, most of which came from China and Japan, though also from Germany, Denmark and Holland. I was particularly drawn to a glass cabinet embedded in the wall at the end of the room. It was filled with a display of Dutch Art Nouveau eggshell porcelain, including two vases with intricate, lively depictions of what looked to be pheasants, and a matching tea set with an elegant teapot at its centre.

I saw Destiny's reflection emerge over my shoulder in the glass cabinet. She asked me about a Japanese incense burner she'd just seen, which took the form of a porcelain rabbit, then launched into a discourse about the challenges she'd experienced writing from the perspective of non-humans in her fiction.

Perhaps, I thought to myself, she had arranged our morning appointment to air questions in response to my talk that she didn't feel comfortable sharing at dinner.

The challenge with writing from the perspective of objects, animals or machines, said Destiny, is that the more we feel ourselves to be withholding our subjectivity from something, the more it seems to creep back in.

Destiny described how she came up against the paucity of her own imaginative resources when trying to find voices for the robots and animals in her work. The best she felt she could do was write a warped or limited version of human psychology into these characters, which to her seemed a passable but somehow inadequate effort to fabricate the sense of a spirit or inner world.

Destiny continued to talk animatedly as we moved into the next room, which contained countless examples of both ancient and modern glassware. The whole time I had the sense there was a subtext to the points she was making, about which I was only partially aware. It felt like there was an invisible third participant in our conversation, perhaps an old combatant, or at least another discussion taking place in her head.

As a consequence, said Destiny, I found myself becoming less interested in questions about non-human perspectives as such, and more interested in how trying to occupy such perspectives led to the elaboration of peculiar forms of humanity or human fantasy.

We moved through a series of progressively darker and more cluttered rooms, which displayed earthenware, large coffins, jewels, measuring devices and forged steel tools, collected—if that is the right word—from Ancient Rome, Greece, Egypt, North Sudan and the so-called Ancient Near East. It was difficult to simultaneously appreciate the profundity of so many beautiful and historically important objects while also participating in what Destiny evidently regarded as a high-stakes discussion. So I was grateful, to some degree, when the appearance of a temporary handwashing station at the end of the exhibit attracted Destiny's attention and talk began to align once . more with an observable, touchable reality.

Destiny squeezed a portion of the liquid into her palm and began rubbing her hands together while reading the infographic.

This is one of the more detailed graphics, she said, inspecting the images closely and then the handwash.

Can you smell the fumes, she continued. This is a reassuringly alcoholic brew. Sixty percent, a desirable quantity of alcohol, which takes it beyond a very strong gin.

I followed Destiny in her handwashing action, experiencing the recently acquired appreciation I'd developed for washing my thumbs and fingertips. The smell of the alcohol, the sensation of the liquid on my hands, and the movement of the hands and fingers themselves awoke something in me to which none of the other museum exhibits had managed to appeal. Destiny informed me that she usually preferred using bars of soap, as they gave her the sense she was actually producing something, namely lather. She found herself increasingly fascinated by the action of wringing and how, when combined with the liquid medium, the firm outline of her hands seemed to dissolve.

I could just go on forever, she said, so recently I've had to introduce a limit of approximately ten rotations to each wash. Otherwise I fear my hands might disappear!

Destiny held out her hand, anticipating the return of a shake, and I only registered the firmness of my own grasp once I'd felt her comparatively cool, loose grip.

Shall we continue? she asked, smelling her hand as it returned to her person as though she might be able to detect the foreignness of my odour against the neutral background of her newly washed skin.

The first exhibit in the next wing of the museum was focused entirely on fruit, or more exactly a sensory exhibit about fruit flesh and skin. There was a section within the fruit exhibit themed 'resistance and transformation' featuring objects that looked and felt like fruit but were synthetic reproductions designed to accentuate particular sensations, in this instance those of a tactile nature. The artists and designers had studied the skin and flesh of fruit in great detail and developed what they described as an entire hypothetical field of research and system of social practices devoted to sensations and substances associated with the sensing of fruit.

We approached the first fruits available for us to touch, bananas and pears, and started to explore their skins by pressing and digging our nails into the flesh.

Destiny described her the simultaneous sense of delight and apprehension she felt in knowing that her impressions would irreversibly damage the skin.

I reflected on this comment for a while and asked whether she thought that the irreversibility of the experience was part of the sensation. In other words, whether it would feel different if we knew and witnessed the immediate and perfect repair of the skins before our eyes.

At least you are asking the right questions, she said.

I continued to ponder the idea as we moved onto the pears, which Destiny and I both agreed were distinctive in their granular composition.

I read out a wall description: *In this imagined world there are lines of products and experiences based on different sensations. People have access to subscriptions for sensations depending on the results of consultations with sensation experts. Various tests are performed to see which sensations are likely to give people the most pleasure and offer the most intrigue. For example, our hypothetical character Joy may have access to granular, grippy, slick and shiny sensations, whereas Tyrone might have access to fuzzy, heady, thick and supple.*

Destiny pressed her long elegant finger into a portion of a pear framed by small Perspex window, which then rotated to a fresh pear after she finished.

She made some comment I only half-heard about the sensation of reconfiguring particles beneath the surface.

We moved into a far larger room, filled with objects that bore no resemblance at all to fruit: strange bloblike shapes, ranging from the size of a human head to a large chair.

Destiny and I drifted apart once again and inspected the different items up close.

I lost myself in the contours of a blob in a Perspex box that at first seemed impeccably cohesive, like glass, then on closer inspection revealed itself to be porous and irregular, like bone or keratin. In this room there were no wall labels, so we were required to speculate ourselves as to the relevance of the objects within this imagined world.

Destiny pointed out that the other blobs didn't have cases, which perhaps indicated this one might be dangerous to touch.

We both looked more closely at the fibres of the blob and agreed that based on what we knew about materials like fiberglass and asbestos, this was a good theory.

Imagine, said Destiny, breathing the tiny particles of glass into your lungs.

It's a beautiful thought, I said, in a way.

The next room contained four objects on a plinth that appeared as though they belonged in your mouth. Mouthguard-type things, I supposed you might call them.

The most striking aspect of these objects was their dusty, mottled surfaces. The mouthguards themselves were a rich purple colour, almost black, and the aforementioned mottling was a bright grey, a kind of mist. The label next to the display invited people to touch the objects but not to put them in their mouth. The label conjectured that there might be a community within a fantasy world where this particular mottled quality was revered as much as the lustre of precious jewels or sexualized attributes of human bodies in the real world.

Destiny knelt down so the objects were at eye level.

It's like the Milky Way, she said. Like looking into a clear sky at night.

These objects incited the desire to bite down on them so strongly that I noticed my jaw clenching.

Destiny asked me what I thought it was that was so inviting about the cloudy surface. She rubbed her thumb lightly across the surface of one of the objects and the cloudy mark seemed to transfigure slightly before returning to the previous pattern.

We lapped the next room quickly and found ourselves back at the entrance of the museum, leafing absentmindedly through pamphlets and the display copy of the exhibition catalogue. Destiny drew my attention to a comment from the editor on the catalogue's front page: *This not so much a record of events as a recreation of them.*

Her finger remained resting next to the text in the catalogue and she blinked, one eye after the other, as though her lids were filling with a light glue. We stood for a while like this, until it became clear I wasn't going to offer a response, and then we descended the small set of stairs to the courtyard outside the entrance, where the sun had returned and an icy wind seemed to herald the worst of the winter months to come.

On the street, in front of the museum, Destiny replaced her cap. I held out my hand, imagining this to be the last time we would see each other. She hesitated, at which point I decided to lean in for a hug.

1. Object Coach

It was my turn to present a project at an event for the university. Unlike the other presentations, which were in the essayistic mode, I decided to tell a story. I wanted to share an account I had composed about an entity called Object Coach, who I imagined might help me during the rehabilitation phase of a hamstring injury.

As had become routine for me, I practiced by reading the story out loud and recording it on my smartphone, which for some reason generated the same feeling as presenting to an audience. I positioned myself at a favoured table in a park by the harbour, underneath a Cottonwood tree, touched record on my device and took a breath, as I had learnt to do, before beginning my story.

Some years ago now, I began, I had seen a physio who gave me a series of strengthening exercises, the intensity of which I was told to gradually increase over time. The exercises involved leaning forward with both my hands against a wall, stretching one leg back, with the other leg on the ground, and then curling my raised leg up at the knee until my heel hit my buttocks, before letting it return slowly to the original straight position. I was to complete four sets of ten repetitions on each leg, adding weights over time to increase the intensity. Initially I wore a riding boot to increase the weight. Then I started fastening small dumbbells to the back of my lower leg with rope and masking tape. But they'd often slip and fall out or dangle down, upsetting my rhythm and balance.

The situation was manageable, barely, but I sensed it could be made a lot easier. I heard of Object Coach from a friend, Patricia, in Brisbane, who had arthritis and found it hard to hold cutlery. She consulted Object Coach after a recommendation from her doctor and had a new cutlery set designed that had large, easy to grip handles.

Patricia had told me about Object Couch during our regular Sunday morning video call. The cutlery set is also beautiful, she said, on one particular call. Let me go and get one for you. I watched Patricia get up slowly from her chair, turn around and shuffle back into the blur of her apartment. She was out of view for some time, long enough for me to put on the kettle and start making a cup of tea.

When Patricia reappeared she presented a knife, a fork and a spoon, with large, red, blue and yellow handles. There's a teaspoon too, she said, it's green, but I could only carry three. They're gorgeous aren't they? I agreed, and not only out of politeness. The designs reminded me of bulky, colourful boomboxes from the 1980s by brands like Sanyo. I noticed two parallel white stripes down the sides of the handles as Patricia rolled them around in her hands.

Blast, she said, as one fell onto the ground and she bent over to pick it up, mumbling something in the process.

No, you must call Object Coach, continued Patricia, when she returned to her chair. Just Google it, she said. Now, letts talk about the tennis. Did you see Rafa last night? Isn't he gorgeous?

I wrote 'Object Coach' down on a post-it note and stuck it to the top of my laptop, where it stayed all week until Saturday morning, when I eventually felt ready to subject myself to some life maintenance. I punched the name into the search bar of my browser. Object Coach was the first page that appeared at the top of the list. I clicked through and it look me to a page with a video playing: a first-person view moving through a 3D visualisation of a house. It reminded me of the computer generated scenes in the films of David Fincher, where the perspective zooms in to trace the hidden electrics that network within the interior. The camera seemed to caress the surfaces and outlines of different objects, whether furniture, electrical goods or accessories, as though its movement was bringing the forms to life.

A chatbox popped up and offered the greeting: *Hi, I'm Object Coach, how can I help you today?* I continued to watch the video as I worked out the best way to describe my injury and exactly what I was hoping the service would offer. *Hi,* I said, unsure whether to use my name. *I'm wondering if you can help me with an injury, well, it's not really the injury but an issue with the rehabilitation process and the exercises I need to perform.*

I began to explain the issue further, with prompts of encouragement delivered from Object Coach. I wondered about the exact nature of the entity at the other end processing my personal information. Were they a human, or a robot, a human using a robot or a robot using a human? Where were they located? What kind of spatial conditions did this thing need to operate?

Whatever the case, the dialogue was peppered with idioms and subtleties of tone that I would expect only from a human. As we continued to converse, I even sensed Object Coach was becoming more familiar, littering our exchange with phrases I associated with those who shared similar cultural and geographical histories as me: *sounds rough, how good, hard to say, ah nice one, good on you, for sure...*

She'll be right fell a little flat, however.

Object Coach said that I would receive a password once I'd paid the service fee, which would allow access to one of the scanners that were popping up around the city with increasingly regularity. Or, if I preferred, I could enable the video camera on my computer and let Object Coach into my house, something I felt was a bit premature at this stage of our relationship.

I went with the password option to start.

I'll send you a form asking for a few details about your medical history and some details about privacy, said Object Coach, *and then I'm sure we'll have you up and running with your hamstrings stronger than ever in no time. Is there anything else I can help you with today?*

I didn't think so.

Yet I had the sense, as I watched the video zoom around what seemed like an endless inventory of objects, that there was probably plenty more Object Coach could offer me.

Once I'd downloaded the Object Coach app on my phone, I could access a map that showed the locations of the scanning booths around the city. It took me a couple of weeks before I eventually got around to going, even though my nearest booth was only a short deviation from my standard route into work. It seemed that for some services, the convenience of spatial proximity didn't influence my practices. It was increasingly challenging for me to muster the desire to do anything outside of work that wasn't an immediate need or didn't bring me immediate pleasure. Despite some level of curiosity, getting a body scan still seemed like a lower priority than getting a croissant or answering emails.

The scanning booths reminded me of other redundant service points scattered around the city, like letter boxes and phone booths. They were everywhere: rectangular green boxes about two metres tall. From a distance it appeared as though they were made from steel but closer inspection revealed they were made from a strange sort of glass. I noticed that despite the scanner looking brand new, it was covered in bird shit and an omnipresent sticky film that seemed to accumulate on things in the city.

I punched my code into the keypad and the two glass doors swooshed open. I stepped inside and immediately appreciated the feeling of the city disappearing and the reduced levels of sensory stimulus. A computer display came to life in front of me: it showed a video loop that I recognised from the Object Coach webpage, then it reconfigured to an image of an androgynous body standing in a booth, which the camera then zoomed in on, so the body became a kind of landscape. The camera panned across the landscape with what seemed to me like a degree of affection.

Hello Tom, good to see you.

Hi, I said. I wasn't sure if I should call the voice Object Coach.

The voice was feminine, with a British accent this time. It reminded me of an actor I couldn't quite place. As the voice explained how the scan would work, it began to stir emotions that made me relaxed, nostalgic and reassured, so that when I began to undress, it felt like a duty I was only too glad to perform. The experience of being naked with little between myself and the outside world was also titillating, though I did have a few cautionary thoughts about past experiences in automated public toilets where the doors opened before I'd finished doing my business.

Once I'd stripped down, Object Coach instructed me to stand on the outline of two feet painted on the floor, which, as I looked down, I realised was a kind of platform.

Put your arms up in the air. Good. Now we're going to spin you around, said Object Coach. I was happy to oblige. The panel swivelled 180 degrees one way and then 180 degrees back.

Object Coach reminded me of a few details about the next stages in the process: I would be able to see a digital prototype version of my devise within two weeks, which I could then personalise before it was printed.

I'll give you more guidance at that point, said Object Coach.

When I re-emerged from the booth, I felt disoriented. Where, exactly, had I just been? When I looked back at the booth it didn't seem accurate to say that I'd simply been in that location. I'd been in another world, a world of rearranged possibilities.

The voice lingered with me for the whole day at work, like a fragment from a dream. Who did it remind me of? The voice felt intimately connected to my past and to certain preferences that were beyond my present powers of articulation. It sounded at once authentic and artificial, familiar and yet alien. I wanted to go back to the booth simply to be in that vibratory womb, naked before the voice. In the typical sense of the word I wasn't 'touched' by Object Coach, however, there seemed no better way to describe the relationship I felt between the surface of my exposed body, that insulated theatre of visual analysis and the sound I'd come to associate with the being I'd imagined was taking my form into its soul.

A week later I received an email from Object Coach with a link to a page where I could view and personalise the device. The 3D visualisation of the design was more stylish than I'd envisaged. It took the form of a kind of sleeve that would fit over the lower half of my leg and allow me to slot in various objects from around the house as weights in my hamstring strengthening exercises—I was thinking mainly books. The device rotated slowly on its virtual platform, and reminded me of a spider web and a shell: part textile, part sculpture. I couldn't help but imagine it was the work of the beautiful soothing voice I'd encountered in the scanning booth.

I played around with the sliders on the interface that changed elements of the design. I assumed at first that these styling options weren't really relevant to my needs. I'd previously thought of using the object exclusively at home, so I wasn't too concerned how it looked. But as I toyed with the design I started to imagine myself actually running with it outside and then finding objects to fit into it if I happened to finish my run in a park or at the beach. I tried to imagine whether there were such appropriately sized loose objects in the locations where I finished my runs and found it surprisingly hard to think of any.

It seemed to me that the part of the city I inhabited was oddly devoid of rocks or branches that were light enough to pick up with one hand but heavy enough to provide some resistance—perhaps, I thought to myself, these are trouble-making objects, cleared away from the increasingly smooth, uniform centres of the urban environment?

There was a 'chat' tab at the bottom of the screen but I didn't feel like engaging with the chatbot version of Object Coach. I clicked on the options menu hoping I might be able speak to the same voice as the one in the booth. There was a voice icon which I clicked, accepting the Terms and Conditions without a thought.

Hi Tom, said Object Coach. What can I help you with?

I was stumped and a little embarrassed at first because I didn't actually need any help.

Do you want help using the interface? said Object Coach. The sliders? The top slider adjusts the...

Even though I didn't really need help with the instructions, I let Object Coach speak and when I'd exhausted the all the troubleshooting advice and I was about to say goodbye, Object Coach asked: Is there anything else I can help you with? We offer an entire range of household and leisure services.

I thought for a while and looked around my room. There were many ordinary problems associated with the routines and products that made up the texture of my life; they were on the tip of my tongue, and I wanted to impress Object Coach with my description of a problem. But in the pressure of the moment, I couldn't bring any to mind.

No, I don't think so.

OK. We'll review your submission and should have the design at your doorstep in less than two weeks.

Almost the second after I ended the conversation an idea popped into my head. I lived in a small, cluttered apartment with limited cupboard space. As a result I used the backs of the two chairs in my lounge room to house clothes that were neither fresh nor dirty. Patricia described them as improvised hat-racks. Toying with the 3D visualisation on the screen had subtly influenced the way I saw the chairs now. Their surfaces seemed less stable. I imagined them as glitchy organic forms, extending in different directions.

Perhaps I could have a chair that was also designed as a hat-rack? Something beautiful that would fit with the other objects in my room, make economical use of the space, and allow me to store semi-clean clothes outside my wardrobe so they could air without touching the clean clothes. There was a whole spectrum of shades between dirty and clean that weren't accounted for in the two extremes of the wardrobe and the dirty laundry basket.

I wanted to contact Object Coach again immediately, but I felt I was being too eager. I knew at an abstract level that Object Coach, whether human, machine or some combination of the two, wouldn't care. It was a service provider, hoping to exploit these kinds of interactions for profit. I assumed that for Object Coach, the underpinnings of my desire to connect were secondary to the information embedded in my communication.

Despite this attempt at rationalisation, I couldn't dispel the uneasy feeling that for Object Coach I was an *object*, which made it a subject, with all the faculties I attributed to subjects, among which interpreting the subtleties of the intentions of other subjects was crucial. And I clearly had, if not a guilty conscience, then at least strong sense that what I wanted from my interactions with Object Coach exceeded the norms of conventional, transactional exchanges. I wanted to immerse myself in that voice and to hear it express approval at the insightfulness of my ideas.

I held off reconnecting with Object Coach and instead, feeling the need to discharge some of my communicative energies, called Patricia.

The first call rang out, as was often the case. She called back shortly after.

I'd initially connected with Patricia when I worked for a volunteer organisation in Brisbane that matched younger people with the elderly. We'd meet for walks around her suburb once every two weeks. I ended up feeling I was getting more out of it than her; she always brought me back down to earth, and I continued to stay in touch after I moved to Sydney. She was sharp as a tack. Her hearing and eyesight were in top order, and she had a new boyfriend, Glen, who I'd often see tottering around in the background while Patricia and I chatted. His hearing and eyesight wasn't as good as Patricia's but he was still very able-bodied, and he took Patricia on expeditions to significant places from her past around the city, to houses where she or her friends used to live.

I told Patricia that I had made good on my promise of contacting Object Coach, as she suggested.

Oh good, good-oh, said Patricia. He's wonderful isn't he. Such a dream.

He, I said?

I was thrown into a spin. Apparently, Object Coach's voice also reminded Patricia of someone from her past. Like me, she couldn't quite place it.

But he can sound quite exotic, said Patricia, at times.

My conception of Object Coach was contingent on certain expectations about the stability of its identity. I could understand it servicing different users, but I found the idea of it becoming a different entity each time unsettling.

That was one concern. The other was how Object Coach managed to be an entirely different voice to both Patricia and I, yet it was the same *kind* of different voice, in the sense that it seemed at once familiar and unrecognisable. Something to which we both warmed.

If I didn't have Glen, said Patricia, I reckon I'd be talking to him all the time.

For the rest of the day I walked around my suburb speculating on the mystery of Object Coach. I had a route that I liked to take along the street where the last of the old weatherboard cottages and brick bungalows still stood, now dwarfed by the apartment blocks that crowded around the train station. It was the second week of spring and unlike much of the weather recently, the temperature felt exactly as it should, warm, with jasmine and wattle bloom in the air, yet retaining a cooler edge. Unlike the increasingly abundant warmer days, the heat was insubstantial, displaced easily by a breeze or patch of shade.

I puzzled at length on the voice of this strange entity. The voice that just moments ago had permeated the little living space carved out from the great rush of the city into which my private life expanded. The voice with whom I wanted to share my ill-formed design ideas, who I wanted to provide me with both discipline and support. A voice that seemed composed of the ephemeral traces of now-forgotten moments of perfection, during which comfort had been supplied through love. A kind of ideal mixture of the romantic and the caring, freshened by something unplaceable, unfamiliar.

I had an emerging theory. The page of Terms and Conditions to which I'd agreed without scrutiny was on my mind. What if Object Coach had access to my search history, old emails, location of birth, social media friends and who knows what else from the vast archive of data to which I added unthinkingly every day? Would that data make it possible to create a voice littered with turns of phrase connected to the vernacular tradition associated with my past and the fantasies into which I spent time breathing life, by watching films, scrolling through images and listening to podcasts, and rising from all this media? Was Object Coach, my ideal voice?

I stopped at the edge of one of the landscaped parks where large gatherings of locals conversed while their dogs crisscrossed the grass. Thankfully the zoning in this part of the suburb had at this point limited the height of new developments to six storeys, so the sun splashed across the green and provided welcome warmth as the cool of the late afternoon began to quickly erode the heat of the day.

As I walked back to my apartment, I felt a different sentiment emerge in response to Object Coach. If it was possible that Object Coach had invented a close approximation to my ideal voice, what else might it be able to create for me using the same information? Who knew what implicit, tentatively articulated needs and desires might be made explicit through the algorithms it used.

My last stop before home was the Moreton Bay figs at the corner of one of the older parks in the suburb. It was once a cow paddock and named after a mayor, who, more than a century ago, had watered the young trees that now formed a vascular border protecting the park from the commotion of the city beyond. Part sporting oval, part informal recreation area, it was even more popular with local dog owners than the previous park. Walking along the path towards the park's centre was like walking a gauntlet, a ceremony in which the human visitor was inspected by packs of canine luminaries.

I loved the dogs but I had come to hear the bats. For as long as I could remember a colony of fruit bats had occupied the fig trees at the periphery of the park. As the daylight disappeared they became raucous.

I could hear them up in the branches of the trees, starting to give voice to the vegetative form. Squawking and readjusting their smooth wings in the darkness.

Sometimes you could see them flying in large numbers across the sky at night, like effervescence released from a dark bottle, a spectacle of some portents. As though there were a party going on somewhere, the destination of which was disclosed on one of the many secret channels used exclusively by these beings of the night.

When I next called Object Coach I decided not to play the antagonistic, disgruntled customer. I had in mind a German word I'd once heard, but which was beyond my capacity to recall accurately enough to spell. It meant 'faith in technology', in the non-human. The example used in this now-forgotten context was getting into an aircraft: every time we fly, we place our lives in the hands of a machine, a profound and often unacknowledged act of trust.

Since my evening walk, I had observed a steadily building urge to subject myself without resistance to the supposed genius of the computing and manufacturing technology with which I had recently been conversing. I wanted to be identified and met generously by a being whose intelligence was different in scope to my own.

Hi Tom, what can I help you with today?

Hi Coach. Well. I wanted you to answer that question for me.

There were traces of a British accent in Coach's voice; perhaps this was a setting determined for provincial Australians such as myself, whose first, much romanticised overseas experiences as an eighteen-year-old were in the so-called old country. The screen showed the now familiar video loop of a domestic interior.

Was this the same room everyone saw? Or was it subtly adapted to my preferences, like Coach's voice?

There's a range of products I can help you with, Tom. I specialise in prosthetics, accessories, small-scale home furnishings, and mementos.

I thought for a while, imagining a cascading list of objects beneath these various abstract categories.

Can you make me something that is *all* of those things?

While Coach paused, I noticed the faintest suggestion of a hum, a soft, static whirr that indicated thinking.

I'll need some more information.

You have all the information you need.

Is it for your house?

Yes. And my body.

And you'd like me devise my own brief?

Yes.

Based on your data.

Yes.

I can do that.

I sensed Coach was already at work while she spoke. As I'd hoped, the feeling I derived from the vision of Coach parsing through my data was deeply pleasurable. I imagined a kind of primal scene where I, chimp-like and vulnerable in my posture, was being groomed.

Coach was busy. I could hear her thinking, composing me as an object of her knowledge. Without thinking, I began to undress, and laid down on my carpet in an imitation of Da Vinci's Vitruvian Man. The barely detectable sensation of the air on my skin was Coach's calculations, her computing caresses, softer than butterfly kisses all over my body.

Is there anything else I can help you with today, Tom?

I wanted to simply lie there on the ground with the interface open, and Coach on the other end of the line. I conjured the image of a candle for Coach's voice, a sonic glow in which I could temporarily bathe; the feeling of being immersed in the perception of another, even when it was detectable as little more than silence.

But I also sensed that leaving Coach on, or open, might also deaden the delight that came from the ephemeral ritual of the call. The snuffing of the candle was necessary to conclude and thereby give final form to the ceremony.

No, that's all I suppose.

The words came reluctantly. I continued to lie on the floor with my eyes closed. I wondered whether I'd behaved in a way that indicated some perverse, abnormal element to my psychology, perhaps this is what I wanted: to be a peculiar customer.

My mystery package arrived one week after the prosthetic for my hamstring exercises. There was a pronounced difference in the quality of anticipation I felt preceding the opening of each package. While I had been excited to see the first evidence of Coach's handywork, the degree of importance that I placed on the mystery package this time was enough to make me nervous.

The box was bigger than I imagined, roughly the size of one of those bulky old flatscreen televisions that occasionally turn up on the side of the road. Although I was aware of the extent to which I was deluding myself, I found it impossible not to regard the package as a gift from Coach, and not just any kind of mass-produced item. This item was different. It was conceived for me, not only in terms of the content of the product—the form it took, the typology to which it belonged—but in terms of the form of thinking that determined the content. In other words, it might have been an entirely new genre of product, something invented due to some obscure need that it was only possible to read once the data of my soul had been interpreted by a virtuoso.

At least was what I told myself as I began to cut into the package with a Stanley knife. Part of me wanted to call Coach to subject her to this revelatory scene. But I sensed that I might want to spend some time alone with the product. And I also knew that something significant about the indirect quality of this communication would be ruined if it seemed as though the virtual Coach was also present in real time.

I stripped down the cardboard to reveal a white, opaque shroud that was made from some anonymous synthetic substance which bizarrely felt wet but not moist. It seemed to adhere to itself through some kind of static compulsion. I unpeeled the form it obscured.

It only started to make sense to me after I'd stepped back, moved around the room to observe it from multiple angles, and then examined it up close, so close it was all I could see. Every part of its surface seemed to warp with figurative details that were impossible to distinguish in a clear and distinct way, but which were intensely expressive, almost animated.

Could I see the background of an image in the ripples of its surface? An image I'd taken long ago and sent to someone in an email? Was there the edge of a lip I remembered from the brother of a girl I loved, which for some reason seemed to evoke my feelings for her more than her own features? I traced my fingers over the surface. At first impression it might have appeared uniform in texture, but every section I inspected with my hands or eyes revealed itself to be subtly different.

Were they little stories from my life attempting to break free from the physical form into which they had been layered? Or was the entire itself a consequence of these expressive details fusing together as one? I wanted to integrate every little lump and depression into my memory so I could inspect them mentally at my leisure.

And then I paused. My fingers brushed over a distinctively smooth region, seemingly blank. It was in the centre of the form, a gentle depression, the surface of which was soft, supple and yet resistant, like my own skin. I brought my face up close. It was the impression of a face, a negative copy of eyes, a nose and a mouth. I brought my own face closer still, until I touched the surface and I could feel my warm breath dissipate between my skin and the object. I pressed my face into the form, a seamless fit. It seemed to soak up my breath. Had I just awoken? What room was this? In what world was my body?

I pressed the circular red stop button on my device and looked up at the previously empty field. Children had emerged from the school across the road and were now scattered at play on the grass. They had been imperceptible to me while I recorded my story, but now their movement and noise filled the air: *five, six, seven, eight,* they chanted, with screams and interjections of *get away, yeah join in too, hey throw the ball,* and occasional queries from the fluoro-vested teachers, whose deeper voices could be heard as they wandered among the different groups. *Five, six, seven, eight...*

2. Meaningful design

I had been invited by Tobe to sit in on some of his classes for a subject called Speculative Design. Throughout the semester he had confided with me about some of the challenges he faced in teaching the subject and the difficulties of explaining the meaning of the words that were central to the learning objectives of the subject.

Presentations of design projects were the culmination of semester. We gathered in a windowless room that was lit with white light. One of the industry judges, who ran her own design agency, had arrived and the other, a senior designer who worked for a large consultancy, was late.

Tobe announced to the class that they should probably begin, as there was a lot to get through.

The assessment for the semester had an exploratory focus. The task was to use a variety of research methods to understand the way smartphones have changed social practices, such as having dinner or going to the toilet, and then to propose an intervention based on this research, which helps people make a better use of their smartphone. Part of the task was determining what *better* was.

Tobe stood in the front of the class and gave an overview of the subject. He first read over the assessment brief, reiterating the marking criteria, which included, among others: *a demonstrated understanding of the relationship between technology, specifically digital interactions, and meaning.*

One of the tools Tobe had used to help explain the importance of meaning was known as the User Experience Hierarchy of Needs. At the top of the pyramid sat the mythic 'Meaningful', at the bottom was 'Functional', then in ascending order: Reliable, Usable, Convenient and Pleasurable.

It sounds more simple than it is, Tobe had told his class earlier in the semester. The lower levels need to be in place for the higher levels to work: meaningful design that doesn't function is a fail.

Nevertheless, he kept coming back to *meaning* over the course of the semester as a way to grade the student work. The students who proposed more straightforwardly functional designs received worse marks and the ones who demonstrated an understanding of meaningful design got higher marks.

After Tobe marked the first assessments, which were undertaken individually rather than in a group, he was pleased to discover a specific example he could use to explain what he had meant by *a demonstrated understanding of the relationship between technology and meaning.*

The assessment required students to visualise sequential frames of action that depicted various mundane events in their lives of people where smartphones played a central role. Each storyboard had nine cells or panels featuring different scenes.

Many of the students focused on how their lives often revolved around the battery life of their phones. Tobe's example focused on the battery icon in the top-right corner of most mobile phones. The storyboard gave an account of how the smartphone user in question, presumably based on the student, didn't like it when the battery icon changed colour to red, indicating battery below 20%. When this occurred, the student would put the phone into low-power mode, so the battery changed colour to yellow.

The key insight in the assessment was expressed in the captions, where the student noted that she didn't actually know how the low power mode worked, she just used it because seeing the battery turn red made her feel anxious and seeing it change back to yellow made her feel relieved.

Here, thought Tobe, is something I can use to explain what I mean regarding the relationship between technology and meaning. He put together a presentation for the class which included highlights and lowlights from the first assessment and when he got to this particular example he began to speculatively develop the insight of the student, suggesting that the next steps would involve exploring different ways to communicate battery life to the phone user, perhaps using different forms of visualisation and digital interactions to highlight subtler, and indeed more meaningful, meanings. Tobe didn't want to give the students any specific suggestions, but he felt confident they would be able to read between the lines and design their own meaningful digital interactions, associated with battery life or any other aspect of the phone they discovered to be important through their research.

Tobe had asked the groups presenting to go in a particular order, with one of the groups he suspected would do well going first. It was a group of four girls. They had a great group dynamic and enjoyed working together.

The group stood before a slideshow presentation and talked about their idea. It soon became apparent the idea wasn't particularly good or easy to understand. Their premise was that people were addicted to social media as facilitated through the use of smartphones, and that this was making people feel lonelier and more depressed. The design proposed by the group enabled users to create what they described as real and genuine social connections. They called their design Connect.

The students showed a video where they acted out archetypal friendship scenarios: going for a walk together, catching up for coffee, looking and pointing at something interesting in the distance. The app they'd designed enabled people to make the most of these occasions without the distraction of a smartphone. The app would send reminders to users that they ought to make the most of a face-to-face encounters if they attempted to use their smartphone in close proximity to another user who had activated the app. For example, if a user took out her phone to check something while at lunch with a friend, if that friend also had Connect activated, a little message bubble would pop up on the screen: *Enjoy hang time with your friend, put me away for later.*

One of the students, a girl in a white roll-neck sweater with navy blue flared pants, stepped forward to describe another feature of the app: a printout record of the user's weekly screen time, which they could obtain by using the mini docket printer that plugged into the phone.

Tobe put his face in his hand in frustration.

This was another feature the students had decided to keep against his advice earlier in the semester. Rather than ditching the idea altogether, the students responded to his advice by emphasising that the printout was made from biodegradable materials.

Tobe snuck a glance at the industry guest who looked on with interest from her solitary position at the judges' table at the front of the room that I assumed Tobe had arranged to lend an air of authority and ceremony to the occasion.

At the conclusion of the presentation Tobe asked if anyone else in the room had any questions. As usual there was deathly silence.

OK, said Tobe, turning to the industry guest. Janelle, do you have any questions for the group? Any advice?

At this point, Tobe realised he hadn't properly introduced his guest, so he interjected before Janelle could respond, said sorry, turned to the class and gave a solemn and ingratiating introduction, emphasising Janelle's influence in the local design industry, her responsibilities within the organisation where she worked and her history of working with the university.

Janelle smiled.

Sorry, Janelle, said Tobe again. Any questions for the group?

Much to Tobe's delight, Janelle picked out the two exact faults he'd emphasised over the semester. She pointed to the naivety show by the students in trying to solve a mobile phone addiction problem with an app, a criticism to which the students responded by smiling wider, more tense smiles.

Janelle recounted a story, a hard lesson for her, when her boss had stamped his foot on the ground, quite close to hers, when she had started on a project with the assumption that the final design would be an app. She echoed the line, to some extent now a truism in the industry: *If you made an app that didn't solve the real problem for the client, then they'd be left with an app and a problem.*

When Janelle questioned the students about the printout, they gave the defence that they'd wanted to combine the analogue with the digital to guide users away from their smartphones and offer another, more meaningful format for communicating important information.

OK, said Janelle, that's cool, but I'm still not sure it really works.

It sounds to me, said Tobe, seeming to enjoy the opportunity for a well-timed bit of advice—it sounds to me like you've included the printer because you liked the idea, but did you do any research to see this is something users would actually use, or whether it's something they even want?

Another student, obscured by her two peers at the front, replied that yes, in fact they had done research. She'd asked a number of people whether they liked the idea of the printer and they said yes.

And did you include details of this in the report, asked Tobe?

Yes we did, replied the student at the front, turning to glance at her peers. It's all in the report.

I really I like the concept behind it, said Janelle, the idea of creating more genuine connections. I just think you could have pushed it a little bit more in terms of how these connections were facilitated, and not relied so much on the phone as the orienting device.

OK, said Tobe. Any other questions?

Tobe said that he hoped the group could see the irony of using a smartphone app to solve a smartphone problem, which he had already pointed out to the group during an interim presentation. He looked to the industry panelist, perhaps to see whether he could register signs of approval in her expression. She was smiling back at the students, showing no outward signs of sympathy.

A final round of applause was offered and the group returned to their seats, looking somewhat deflated. Tobe said that for the next group he would nominate a respondent group, so there would be at least once question from the class.

The next group presented their design for an interactive dinner table that aimed to encourage face-to-face conversation. A key feature of their design was a shallow lip or shelf that ran around the lower edge of the table. Here users could place their smartphones, so as to invite particular changes in the atmosphere of the room, particularly to do with light and sound, that were triggered through the table.

The group showed a video of a product demonstration where they acted out the role of a nuclear family having dinner. The family appeared to live in a small apartment, with a dining table in the kitchen. The camera focused on the expressions and gestures of the characters, who were presumably meant to be children, there was little to distinguish the characters from how the students appeared in real life. The children were bored. They used their smartphones in a distracted and deflated fashion, with glum faces and slouched postures. The parents, who had been busy preparing and serving dinner, were clearly frustrated when they sat down at the table to eat dinner with their distracted children. Then the video froze. There was a loud sound effect and animated lightning bolts smashed through the roof of the small apartment, shocking the family. The children spilled noodles on their clothes and the parents placed their hands on their faces in awe. A young woman (one of the students) appeared in the foreground of the screen and started to introduce their product, called 'Time Home'.

The video cut to a new scene showing the family sitting around their interactive dining table instead. The children now appeared to be animated by convivial energy and the parents were no longer frustrated. The parents placed their phones on the little shelf that ran around the lower edge of the table and the children followed. As soon as all four phones were on the ledge, the table turned dark black and a luminous green line traced its way around its edge before appearing on the surface of the table in a dance of knotting and unknotting forms. The family laughed joyously at this display and lent backwards on their chairs. The light above the dining table gradually brightened, then flashed, obliterating the entire room, before dimming again, revealing the figures at the table in more subdued lighting. They lent forward to enjoy their food, smiling and looking at each other in the eyes while they ate.

At the conclusion of the video the class erupted into loud applause. Tobe, who I imagined might have been unsure about the presentation, couldn't help but join in. Janelle smiled and looked at Tobe while she clapped. Tobe shrugged his shoulders.

Well, said Tobe, I'm not quite sure how to respond to that video. I suppose the reaction of the class speaks for itself.

Janelle interjected: I think you've got the tone just right, it's very unique. I mean, I'm tired of being serious, and you've hit on something really great here. It's very redeeming, you know, we can tell you're not being serious.

Both the tutor and the guest commented favourably on the shelf affordance on the table, which they agreed was a distinctive feature, around which a compelling product might potentially be designed.

It's simple, said Janelle, but in a way quite profound. Why don't we have more tables with these kinds of shelves, particularly if they have the kind of digital interactivity you're proposing?

There's a risk, isn't there, said Tobe, that the table might in itself become a distraction?

We thought of that, said a short student with dark hair who stepped outwards, as though protecting the rest of the group. The table is designed only to offer a short entertainment, at the beginning, and then the family can play together to increase social interaction. Like with a board game.

The student had a point, conceded Tobe, who then shared an anecdote about the various games he'd played with his family growing up, and how cards in particular was still something that bought their family together in a manner that he could only describe as meaningful, perhaps more meaningful than the meal itself. Tobe said he was unsure why responded differently to the idea of a digital game, which was part of an interactive table, that a family might play together—was it simply a prejudice based on his own childhood using analogue games?

When Tobe looked to the rest of the class for comment, he realised he had forgotten to allocate a respondent student group. He singled out a relatively confident student from the group that presented earlier and asked whether she had any questions about the presentation.

The student echoed the views of the tutor and industry guest about the shelf and emphasised that she loved the video. Echoing the feedback her group had received, she posed the question as to whether the design might make the family more dependent on their phones.

You need the phones to be on the shelf for the table to work, right? Wouldn't that, potentially, make the family more reliant on their phones?

The short student with dark hair once again stepped to the front of the group and on this occasion began a difficult-to-follow defence of the idea. It wasn't clear whether his response was a refutation of the premise that having the phones at the table was a bad thing, or whether he agreed with the premise and was attempting to explain how the design mitigated the issue.

The longer the student talked the more confusing his discourse became, until Tobe, perhaps unable to deal with the cognitive stress of following the student's logic, or out of embarrassment with Janelle's presence in mind, or simply due to time constraints, suggested they move on to the next and final group.

The student, however, persisted in responding to the question and now started to refer to research the group had conducted that, while not seeming relevant in the slightest, apparently supported his view that their design had been mindful of the potential shortcomings highlighted by the questioner.

Tobe at this point had to put his foot down and referred to the talking student by his first name, requesting him to finish and to take a seat, the rest of his group having done this already. The student took this well and, having awoken from the strange justificatory trance into which he'd fallen for the last few minutes, walked to his seat with a proud smile and was received by the rest of his group with congratulatory pats.

The final group was a composed of four young men, all students from abroad except one. Their design was, like the other groups, based around the idea of encouraging more genuine connections between people. In this case they had decided to propose their idea as a modification of a popular existing social media site, which in their eyes had become antisocial.

It was clear early in the presentation that the four boys had quite close over the course of their project. They spoke with conviction about this problem with which they had direct acquaintance. There was a sense of the group functioning as a therapeutic structure; the young men often touched each other on the backs and shoulders and nodded knowingly at points, as though they'd shared stories of great emotional significance. Unlike the other presentations, the group didn't include a video, and instead used photographs of the group on research field trips, where they had posed for the camera as though on holiday.

At this point the second industry guest arrived, looking particularly wired after a long day of work. He took a seat at the back of the room, rather than next to Tobe and Janelle at the front, presumably on account of not wanting to disturb the presentation. Tobe immediately cued into his presence and glanced back often while the presentation continued.

The group proposed an alternative icon and name for a digital interaction that enabled users of the social media service to indicate whether they approved of various bits of content other people shared on the site. The icon was called 'embrace' and the group suggested the interaction it symbolised expressed a greater warmth of emotion than existing icons of its type used on social media. They argued that it would allow for and encourage users of the site to engage in a manner that was more heartfelt.

At the conclusion of the presentation, the faces of the students were taut with hope, their foreheads glistened in the bright overhead lighting and they stood waiting to receive a judgement that would either carry them off on a wave of uplifting emotion or brutally crush them like a heavy stone.

Tobe turned to the industry guest that had come in late and offered another praiseworthy introduction, emphasising how busy the guest must have been with his other work and how fortunate the students were to have him in the room.

Do you have any questions or comments for the group? asked Tobe.

As the industry guest started to talk, a certain brightness started to fade from Tobe's face. According to the industry guest, the students had struck gold with the 'embrace' concept and accompanying icon. He was convinced, in fact, as he had just been working with the large social media company referenced in the presentation.

Sometimes, said the guest, apparently incremental changes were the changes of greatest significance.

People in industry are tired, said the guest, looking around the room with a sense of confidence and conviction that typically comes from personal experience with a problem—people in industry are tired of design companies coming to them and proposing radically new solutions that don't go anywhere. It's no good proposing a new paradigm—he was sick of the word 'paradigm'—if it's not feasible to implement. There are so many beautiful ideas, grand, revolutionary, charismatic, sexy ideas that are gathering dust in a top drawer somewhere.

At this point Tobe looked to Janelle, who appeared to be nodding along.

The industry guest continued his diatribe, declaring that the idea that incremental change can't be significant was wrongheaded. He believed there were implicit, spatial metaphors at work that delude people: revolutions can go nowhere, can go backwards. But little can be big, the increment can trigger a cascade of changes that are difficult to predict.

It doesn't always work, necessarily, said the guest, but some small changes, with the right strategy, can get a real foothold. Sometimes, you've got to cut with the grain to get stuff done. Otherwise you're continuously fighting an uphill battle. Just spinning your wheels.

I'm sorry but I have to agree, chimed Janelle. I mean, this has been on my mind a bit recently.

Janelle described how she was talking to one of her clients the other day about a previous design agency they'd worked with, a number of years ago, which had presented this really captivating work.

All the staff in the client's organisation really got behind it, emotionally, you know, said Janelle. But in the end, what ended up changing? Nothing. It made everyone happier for a while, and maybe a few tiny details had changed. But they were the wrong tiny details. Design needs to be more strategic and less...less design.

Tobe interjected and drew attention to a specific aspect of their design. He noted that he appreciated how they'd stripped back the visual elements in their example design and focused on what was important, which in this case was the written dialogues generated between different users. Tobe added, with some hesitation, that he was still a little unsure about the idea that changing the interaction to embrace would have the impact they'd imagined.

It might, he said, but it's something you'd have to test. Actually, this is a good lesson for all the groups. Try and identify what they key assumptions are in your ideas and then work out compelling ways to test them. That's where most of the design work is, not in the final product. The final product is important. But if you want a really strong idea, you need to do the research through testing.

We've said it all semester, continued Tobe, looking to his guests for the approval they immediately gave with firm nods of agreement.

Pleased with the level of engagement from his guests and the general atmosphere of the room, Tobe then turned to the other students, realising he'd once again forgotten to nominate a respondent ground.

Sorry. Sorry. I forgot to nominate a group again, he said. Does anyone have any questions? We're not ordering pizza until someone asks a question.

There was a long silence, before one student offered the opinion that he liked the photographs the group had included to demonstrate the research they did together, less on account of the authority they lent to the design process and more due to the sense they gave that the group had had fun, at which point the group, who until that point had frozen like statues in postures of strained openness and pride, seemed to collectively shudder with vibrations of relief and began to move again, turning to each other with smiles of agreement and casual affection.

3. Del & Zep

One of my nominated duties as a design academic was to bring together literary fiction and design research as a new genre of writing, or less ambitiously, a different sensibility. I was pleased to discover that one of my colleagues, Del, was now writing fiction. For once one of my colleagues was a stranger in my disciplinary domain. Perhaps I could be of assistance, I thought.

Del had a background in industrial design and the story she was working on described the lives of a group of creatives from her profession, who had been marginalised in a world dominated by engineers and mathematical reasoning of a particularly restrictive variety.

The plot, so Del told me, was very loosely inspired by the TV series *Mad Men*.

I'd shared a story I wrote about 3D printing with Del and her friend Zep earlier in the year. Zep had a background in fashion and textiles and worked in the same research space as Del. They were often seen doing things together, both professional, research-related things in the lab where they worked, and casual friend things like having lunch in the university cafeteria.

The story I'd shared was Object Coach and, as I told Del and Zep in my email, it was in part modelled on my debut novel, the plot of which involved a relationship between a young runner and his coach, a woman called Coach Fitz. I liked the idea of the coach figure as an archetype; a kind of tool in my toolbox that I could redeploy in different contexts to obtain new insights.

On this occasion, the coach figure in my story was an indeterminate being, by which I mean, a being that might have might have been human, machine or some combination of the two. I deliberately kept my descriptions of the character allusive, to allow people to form their own ideas about the peculiar agency of this figure—one of the advantages, I thought, of certain kinds of written texts.

I didn't receive any communications from either Del or Zep after I emailed my story, so I sent them a further email to organise a meeting in the space where they worked, known as the Protolab, which is when Del told me about her *Mad Men*-inspired story.

I had an ulterior motive for this meeting. I was planning to use my encounter and communications with Del and Zep in another short story that involved a quasi-autobiographical narrator figure, called Tom, meddling in the romantic lives of two characters based on Del and Zep. My story came at this familiar narrative conceit from an oblique trajectory. Rather than being about matchmaking and romance, my story was really about the manipulation of reality: the efforts of an author manipulating reality by translating it into fiction; the efforts of Tom within the story, who attempts to manipulate characters based on Del and Zep; and the characters of Del and Zep themselves, who, as designers, were using 3D printing to manipulate reality in the objects they made.

Such an approach to storytelling, I wrote to Del and Zep in my initial email, is less to do with fictional characters as fully formed, psychological individuals who encounter each other in a fictional world, and more to do characters and narratives as projects, beings of a contingent reality, explicable as problems of design.

When I first arrived in the Protolab, however, Zep wasn't around, it was just Del, a high school student doing work experience, and four or five other designers working on desktop computers. At least two were refining 3D models of objects, one a canoe, the other was indeterminate. I was at once hyperattentive to my surrounds and what Del said, and yet vaguely removed from the immediate rhythm of events, as was common when absorbing experiences for my fiction writing.

Del gave me a quick tour of two of her current projects. She was exploring the design possibilities of carbon fibre and looking at circuit boards and wearable technology. She was also creating a glass lamp for a gallery modelled in part on the form of the common schooner glass.

I mentioned that I'd seen photos Del had taken of seaweed on her Instagram feed. I had a vivid image of the different textual qualities expressed in these images in my mind as she continued to explain the project to the student and I. Del was specifically interested in the high levels of responsiveness seaweed had to rehydration.

Yes, I affirmed, I remember taking some bunches from the beach and laying them in our pot plants. They'd dry out, and then whenever we'd water the garden the seaweed would be significantly revived by the liquid.

I asked a few more questions about the carbon fibre project while we stood behind one of the designers, who was working on canoe visualisations on a desktop computer. Del explained that designers often didn't work with carbon fibre. It was perceived to be a difficult material. Engineers were typically the most common users of carbon fibre and there wasn't an history of using it the industrial design community. Del was hoping to obtain knowledge of the material through intensive, hands-on experimentation, and then combine this with a design sensibility aimed at using material in a way that was more targeted to the needs of users.

Take car side-mirrors for example, said Del, they are often made from carbon fibre, despite not exploiting any of its unique material qualities.

Del explained that making flexible hinges was a better use of the material, and expressed this by evoking the form and affordance of a stretchable hinge gesturally with her hands.

We sat down together on a couch in one of the lab's cordoned-off meeting spaces, at which point Del, asked, somewhat abruptly: how can I help you Tom?

I had prepared a response to this question and began by describing my research ambitions relating to fiction and design, which I compared to science fiction in the sense that I was trying to give voice or a sense of being to technologies.

Though I suspect most readers of science fiction would in the end be very disappointed and perhaps even angered by my work, I said to Del, if they happened to be enticed by the higher-level comparison with the genre.

I was hoping you might agree to being a character in the story, I said, half-jokingly. All you need to do is meet with me a couple of times at specific locations around the university.

Del seemed enthused by the idea, though I didn't feel as though I'd left her much choice.

We then talked about the tendency of science fiction to be dystopian and the value of emphasising how much the future is shaped by the past. Del used the example of living rooms in the Edwardian period being filled with Victorian furniture.

Exactly, I said, glad that there was a shared level of understanding between us.

At that point Zep came in.

Tom's just chatting about the story he's writing, said Del.

Del can tell you all about writing stories, said Zep, she's working on one herself. Like *Mad Men* but design.

Really? I said.

Zep, you've really dropped me in it there, haven't you?

What's it about? I asked.

It's only... said Del. I only just started writing it. More as a venting exercise.

Venting about being a designer working with engineers. The frustrations you encounter.

Del then proceeded to tell me a story about a table she designed.

When I told the engineers at the prototyping space about the idea, said Del, they didn't want to be involved, they dismissed it, said it wouldn't work. But I knew, because of my experience, I knew it would work. Now they want me to show it off as something they can do with their technology. And I don't know if I want to let them show it off.

And how does that fit in the story, I asked?

Well, said Del, there's this future world where creativity isn't valued, where only science, maths and technology are taught, and the product designers, kind of like in *Mad Men*, are this underground group, sought after and vilified at the same time.

It takes a special manufacturer to realise the value of design, continued Del, and then when they do they make a real impact, like the MX3D 3D-printed steel bridge. If engineers build a bridge, there's this set way you do it. You put up the trusses—it's not a bridge unless it's engineered like a bridge, and that has been predetermined. I'm generalising here, I realise. You should check it out the bridge.

It turned out that Del hadn't even read the section of *Object Coach* I'd sent her. Zep had read it. He mentioned that he liked my descriptions of the 3D scanning infrastructure that were dotted around the city— kind of like old payphone booths—and particularly how the booths got covered in ibis shit.

On my way out of the research lab, I stopped to look at the table Del had mentioned in our chat. It was displayed on a large plinth next to the window, so it was visible to the pedestrians who walked past the lab. There was a booklet propped up next to it explaining the idea and the technology used in the design. The design of the table was based on combining Del's fingerprint with some of the designs of Lucien Henry, an artist and artisan who spent twelve years in Australia in the late nineteenth century and was among the first European artists who used natural flora and fauna in his artworks and designs. Del used some of Henry's design as the basis for the form of the table, which looked a little like a tree stump, with the grooves of the fingerprints resembling the curved, interlocking grains of growth rings in wood. The closing sentence in the booklet described the design as a mixture of manual and digital processes, with the initial fingerprint impressions expressed through ink on paper, digital scanning, 2D vector tracing, and 3D CAD using the software program Solidworks.

I found a café and started to write everything I could remember from the meeting. I realised I needed to organise more actual meetings with Del and Zep to acquire more material for my match-making story.

Initially my interest in the actuality of their romantic connection had been trivial—if that's the right word. I primarily wanted to see if I could make something believable happen in the fictional world of my story and acquire material for this purpose. Over time I started to invest more and more in the idea. Even so, I felt that my attachment was ultimately ephemeral, despite its paradoxically inflated, temporary importance. Like many of my projects: simultaneously captivating and transitory.

The idea of setting Del and Zep up wasn't just appealing because of this conceptual interest, however. I wasn't interested in match-making *any* two people. I was drawn in by some notion of compatibility between them. This vague sense of rightness and the potential to make things right, no matter how deluded I might be, reminded me of the flames that used to burn within me when looking for love in my younger years. I suppose I was trying to rekindle these flames, by proxy.

I set about contriving a date where Del, Zep and I could observe the sandstone carvings at NSW Technical College, a late nineteenth-century building designed by W.E. Kemp in the Romanesque Revival style; one of my favourite buildings in Sydney. The carvings featured Australian flora and fauna in beautiful motifs that reminded me a little of the Lucien Henry designs that had inspired Del's table.

I started to imagine and write about romantic encounters between Del and Zep quite often. The standard context for these so-called encounters was a camping trip at coastal location organised by one of their mutual friends. It was important that they got to know each other outside the workplace. Del would drive up by herself on her motorbike. The rest of the group was already there, settled in.

On the first night, Del and Zep wouldn't really connect. They'd spend their time talking to other people. But then on the second night, after Zep cooked beans on the fire for everyone, they'd sit next to each other and start to chat about design. Del would feel a growing sense of affection for Zep as they talked. She would think of this moment in the weeks after: his face illuminated in the soft light of the fire, a slightly crooked tooth making his lower lip extend outwards slightly as he talked, and his remarkable ability to grasp even her most awkwardly expressed ideas and speak them back in a clearer, more elaborate form. They would talk about the difference between working as a designer and researching design at a university, and their mutual love of outdoor activities: for Del, surfing and for Zep, bike riding.

In retrospect the Del character would be stunned that she didn't even pay any attention to Zep on the first night. She might have said hi to Zep, among other pleasantries, but he hadn't seemed important to her. But on the second night, Zep had left an impression that would not only define Del's memory of that weekend, but her purpose in life for the next year, as bizarre as that seemed.

I imagined the group of friends going for a swim on the morning of the last day camping. I pictured Del swimming in a group with Zep and two other friends, Tyrone and Clancy, who were a couple. They were trying to catch the little waves, enjoying the beautiful ambience of the beach and the tree-covered headlands that spilled down into the water at either end, which gave Del a sense of safety and adventure at the same time.

It wasn't ideal saying bye out in the water but Del needed to drive back to Sydney for dinner with her dad. She'd either have to settle for a distant, verbal goodbye or hug people in waist-deep the water, wet skin on wet skin, which seemed too intimate.

Well, I've got to head home, said Del, deliberately to the whole group, rather than just Zep—she didn't want to reveal the greater sense of intimacy she felt towards him.

OK, said Tyrone, see you later then.

Del waded over to Tyrone in the water and gave him a hug. Clancy was further out so Del didn't bother. Del waded back across to Zep and hugged him goodbye, her wet cheek against his, the water a second skin, a shared body between them, electrified by their closeness.

I enjoyed our chat last night, said Zep.

Me too, said Del.

My idea of inviting Del and Zep on a walk around the NSW Technical College to admire some of the stone carvings took on a certain definiteness and weight over time. I soon found myself drafting an email to them, from the same table where I'd written about their fictive meeting on the camping trip up the coast. I asked whether they'd like to meet for lunch or coffee one day next week.

I'll make a cake, I wrote, *or if we do lunch I'll make some sandwiches—let me know of any dietary requirements. I look forward to catching up.*

Del was the first to respond to my email. She said that she'd love to catch up and asked about how my 3D printing story was going. *Unfortunately my writing on the Mad Men story has stalled,* she wrote. Though not, apparently, due to lack of material: Del had started working closely with some engineers on a recent project and wondered whether *the idea of being adopted by the engineers as an outsider will help the plot of any future writing of these stories.*

I noticed Del had been posting more images of kelp on her Instagram feed: a small knot of the seaweed in her hand, then floating in a white porcelain bowl, the seaweed extended like large, slippery strips of pappardelle. She'd also posted some of her experiments with carbon fibre, specifically foldable carbon fibre laminate. Some of the comments on her images suggested ideas for packaging and a further affirmation that carbon fibre wasn't a well-understood material in the industrial design community. In the background, scattered over the desk, I noticed drawings of a canoe.

Zep eventually responded as well. I wondered whether he'd been avoiding contact on account of feeling sheepish for not having responded to the other random emails I'd sent him in my attempt to obtain biographical information I could use my story, though it was more likely he was just busy.

Once Del and Zep had confirmed, I started to visualise the event more clearly and decided, with some reluctance, that it would be far better if the meeting took place at dusk, rather than in the harsh light of lunchtime. So I wrote out another email, making an excuse about having something on that day, and asked *if it would be possible, but please don't feel any pressure, if we could move the occasion to the early evening of the same day?*

I decided it would be ideal if I was deliberately late to the meeting, so Del and Zep might have the time to chat before I arrived. To my annoyance, when I walked down from work to the entrance of the NSW Technical College on Mary Ann St, which I'd specified as the meeting point, only Zep was waiting, wearing an informal, scruffy outfit, with thongs, very dirty feet and a really stupid hat. He seemed pleased to see me, disarmingly so, and I wondered, in the context of this different emotional resonance, whether I'd really *got* him during the couple of years we'd known each other. He induced a feeling that made me immediately want to confess everything and explain my plotting—this was conveyed more through his smile and eyes than anything specific he said. We talked distractedly about the NSW Technical College and our present concerns associated with work. Zep said, 'Umm…' a lot, in a vaguely Irish accent, and it seemed part of the song of his voice, rather than a distracting pause.

So, I imagine things are starting to get busy now for you, with teaching? When does semester start? he asked.

It's next week, actually, we're in Orientation week. O week—there's three of them now.

Three, really. Oh.

And how's things with you, how are all the projects going?

Del didn't come to the meeting that day. She gave an excuse that for some reason I refused to believe, about another meeting with an industry partner going overtime. I was furious with her for an hour, then moved on. My desire to confect a romance between them also more or less completely dissipated after that, though, in one last gesture of fidelity to the idea, I decided to send an adapted version of my matchmaking story a couple of weeks after the failed meeting at the NSW Technical College, with both Del and Zep included in the one email.

I faced one particular dilemma, in terms of whether to alter certain details of my story: the issue of my irritation at Zep's outfit on the day of the meeting, which I'd included as the final scene in the story, most conspicuously his hat. I decided to shift my focus from aesthetic judgements about his outfit, to descriptions of his face, and here not so much isolated attributes associated with the shape of his eyebrows, hairline, jawline and so on, but more its topological aspects, like the relationship between his cheek and lips and how his skin looked in the evening light. I tried to make it seem as though my description was at once highly specific, yet common to all faces.

Eventually Zep replied to my email. *Thank you for trusting me with this*, he wrote, *and sorry it took so long for me to get back to you. I was strangely nervous while reading, like watching a film of yourself. You write with an enjoyable cadence, it's honest and engaging. I don't really know what to do next...*

I didn't hear from Del until a year later, after she'd started working at another university, when I sent her another email asking for a few more details about her *Mad Men* story. She made no reference to my story, which made me suspect she hadn't read it, and told me once again she hadn't worked on her story for some time. On this occasion her description of the conceit made no reference to *Mad Men*:

Hi Tom,

Great hearing from you, I'm flattered that the short discussion about my story struck such a chord!

The story I was writing was intended to be a sci-fi dystopia, an end-of-the-world type of thing with a heroine who discovered this 'power' to be creative in a world where the engineers had won, and where creativity had been eliminated from society through education, etc. The idea is there's no place for creativity in this world where data, analysis, algorithms and AI can solve every problem. I think this storyline resonates for me now more than ever, since 'design' at my new job is all about optimisation, not humans, needs, creativity...as you can imagine many people here view those of us who call ourselves designers as being weird, different, and not really part of the school. Writing this to you makes me want to get back into writing my story!

4. The terror of mirrors

With the teaching semester underway, I soon found students demanding examples of what I meant by vernacular design projects. Rather than provide definitions or theoretical examples as I had done in the past, on this occasion I conceived an unusual experiment undertaken by a character called Morgan, who had developed an antagonistic relationship with mirrors. As I imagined the germ of this story, I started to write it down, and in writing the story become more intricate and expansive. Then I spoke the story into my smartphone, rewrote it again, recorded again, then I shared both the recording and the text with the some of my colleagues, hoping they might offer some feedback before I trialled the approach at scale on the students.

Morgan had been researching mirrors for a talk he was giving on the human face and he'd become convinced by the idea that they'd had a very damaging effect on our psychology.

The terror of mirrors, he'd say, describing them as ego-technical media. Morgan spoke in florid terms about a blissful time before mirrors, where people lacked an image they confidently believed corresponded to what others saw of their face.

I questioned him softly once or twice as to whether we could really place that much weight on such a simple technology—weren't mirrors answering a need that humans had known for many centuries as narcissism? But Morgan would raise his voice at such conjecture.

arguing that cheap, well-made glass mirrors afforded a particularly intense variety of narcissism at a hitherto unprecedented scale.

A scale, he said, that qualified as a difference in kind not just in degree.

At that point I went back in my shell. What did I know about how people felt before the 16th century?

All this reading and thinking and reflecting led to Morgan deciding that it was time for him and his partner, Kieran, to do away with mirrors in their apartment.

At first, he said, I thought I'd just paint them over with black, but I decided it wouldn't look very nice having large, painted black rectangles on the wall in the bathroom and bedroom.

So instead, Morgan decided to remove the mirrors entirely. When he proposed this idea to Kieran initially she agreed. Then, after some thought, Kieran suggested that she might on occasion like to use a mirror herself.

Can't you use your phone, said Morgan, or the window?

After further discussion about the specifics of Kieran's needs, the two came to an arrangement whereby Morgan would make himself available as a service for photographing Kieran at her request, should she need the advice provided by an image of her face or figure.

Morgan found he had no trouble removing and divesting the small mirror in the bathroom, for which he felt little affection. When it came to the large, wood-framed mirror in the bedroom he found himself hesitating. He'd been left with the mirror after a previous breakup and while he hadn't thought of himself as being sentimentally attached to it, now he discovered that it meant something to him. He looked at his face through its flecked, sliver surface as though some vestige of his spirit were sedimented there.

Morgan puzzled over how he would accommodate his desire to emancipate himself from the terror of so-called ego-technical media with these opposing feelings of attachment to his personal history. He decided that instead of leaving the mirror leaning against a tree on the grass verge outside the front of the apartment complex as he'd imagined doing, he would request that his neighbour Natalie, with whom he was quite friendly, keep the mirror in her apartment.

Natalie was familiar with what her and Kieran mockingly called Morgan's 'ideas'. She complied with his proposal since it was, after all, such an elegant mirror. She gave it a bit of a clean and leant it at a very slight angle against the wall in her bedroom.

Four days later Natalie heard a knock at her door. It was Morgan, looking dishevelled. He wanted to know whether he could possibility, for no more than a few seconds, sneak a look in the mirror as today was the occasion of his talk on the human face. It was a large public gathering and he wanted to ensure the ensemble of his pants, shirt and jumper all matched.

I've been trying, said Morgan, to get the same effect from car windows, photos that Kieran takes and even video, but it's just not the same.

Natalie suggested that he might like to take the mirror off her hands entirely if this was going to become a habitual request. Morgan assured her that it was one time only, and, once Natalie nodded, he proceeded to wander through her living room and into the bedroom to look in the mirror. As soon as he stood there before it, he wondered why he'd come. There was no real need.

Over the next few weeks Natalie saw more of Morgan than she had in the past two years. Every second or third day he would either send an apologetic text or come knocking at her door to request a look in the mirror. At first he bothered with elaborate excuses, these however were soon replaced by increasingly parsimonious communications, culminating either in a pre-emptive 'thankyou' or the word 'mirror' followed by a question mark.

On account of these extra communicative hurdles, Morgan found himself building a new relationship with the mirror. He enjoyed feeling a mild titillation on account of making peculiar demands of Natalie, the look and the smell of her apartment, the different light in her bedroom, and, perhaps most of all, saying '*mirror?*' to himself in a deep, infantile voice as he composed his texts.

The arrangement had also provoked something in Morgan's thinking that had started to change his attitude and theories about the place of mirrors in the history of human psychology. Rather than spend time tracing over and adding detail to his convictions that mirrors had been a pernicious force, he started to imagine different service models for the access of mirrors around which new social relations might be built. His experiment with the mirror in Natalie's apartment had triggered a whole range of hypothetical wonderings about civilisations where mirrors were only in public places, or where, upon purchasing a mirror, customers were provided with a script for a set of psychologically beneficial practices of looking, such as particular incantations to accompany the moment when one observed one's own face. Morgan found himself singing songs and adopting peculiar gestural routines in the mirror in Natalie's room, to give further colour and scope to these speculative imaginings.

He recalled two crows that used to play in the mirror in the garden of Kieran's parents' old house. As soon as there was enough light in the day, the birds would flock to the mirror, which lent against the fence in order to give the illusion of space. They must have been waiting in the trees nearby for the reflective surface to become luminous enough for the games they played with their doubles. Their hard beaks made a distinctive sound against the glass that reverberated throughout the rooms of the house. Morgan used the word 'clacking' to describe this sound. *Clacking*, definitely not 'clanking', which sounded too metallic. He'd say the word in his mind, making no perceptible audible noise but still satisfying himself with the thought that the word perfectly captured not only the specific noise the birds made, but also the distinctive materiality of beaks coming together with glass.

One day, Natalie took an unusually long time to answer after Morgan knocked on her door. He was smug with the feelings he'd come to associate with the beginning of the little routine. He was just about to write her another 'mirror?' text, when the front door opened and Natalie stood there, one arm around his mirror as though it were a misbehaving adolescent she'd decided to eject from her abode. Morgan understood the deal, and without a word he took the mirror and walked it back to his apartment, facing it away from his body so that he couldn't indulge in the reflection until a deliberate, orchestrated moment, as had become his habit.

Morgan sat for a while on the end of his bed, wondering what to do with the mirror. Things couldn't go back to normal, he was certain of that. But he wasn't willing to follow through with his original plan and get rid of the mirror either.

When Kieran returned from work later that day she found Morgan trying to shunt a towel-wrapped mirror into the lower level of the wardrobe. Morgan had spent the day deciding which towel would be the most appropriate covering for the mirror. He found the different feel of the towels pressed against the slick, shiny surface of the glass enticing. A heightened desire to protect the mirror emerged as he imagined it enfolded in the soft, fibrous towels. Colour too suddenly took on an unanticipated importance, and the turquoise towels on which Morgan eventually settled triggered a feeling of satisfaction when he imagined the cloth in contrast to the silver sheen of the mirror. *How is it*, he pondered, *that we can say mirrors are silver and yet they appear to be filled entirely with the colours of the images they reflect?*

Sadly, for both Morgan and Kieran, the mirror didn't fit in the wardrobe. It was just a little bit too big, so he left it there, jutting out, partially exposed under the two turquoise towels. Morgan was broken by the effort. He was out of ideas and now vaguely hostile to the mirror, which represented the despair that often came at the conclusion of one of his little projects, whether or not he perceived himself to have been successful in its execution. He imagined layering the surface of the mirror in substances or veils of a gradually increasing opacity until its reflective powers were obliterated. And then he imagined smashing the mirror while it was blinded by the cloth, its shards splintering into a further, more permanent blindness.

Kieran was too familiar with scenes of this type to pay it much heed and instead, as had become customary when she came home from work, she asked Morgan if he would be able to take her picture from a low angle on the ground once she got changed into the outfit of her choice.

***

Beta was the only colleague who contacted me in response to my story.

This is perfect, she wrote.

At the time I had no idea what Beta meant by 'perfect'. Perfect in what sense?

Some weeks later, when we met in a cafe near the campus, she started to explain. Like most of my colleagues at the time, Beta wore only black. I also noticed she had the remarkable ability of gathering flecks of food all over her face.

Your protagonist, what's his name again?

Morgan, I said.

Morgan. The moment he decides to get rid of the mirror he's beginning a quasi-design brief, albeit unintentionally. There's a set of everyday routines that he's disrupting by getting rid of the mirrors. And then the rest of the drama in the story emerges from the various prototyping exercises associated with it. As you hint, he's exploring a new service model at a conceptual level for the access of mirrors; he's creating new forms of social life by engaging his neighbour and the photographing service that he performs for what's her name—

Kieran.

Kieran, said Beta, and what I like, at least from the perspective of reading fiction, is that things don't go as planned. The specific materiality of the mirror too, continued Beta, it mixes with Morgan's imagination and generates these sense-substance or sense-material mental events. The narrative reminded me of how the everyday can be moulded in lots of different configurations. The story gives you an idea of how malleable, how changeable things are that might otherwise appear routine or fixed.

Beta continued on. When I was reading, I started to imagine different objects substituting for the mirror, such as a smartphone. In a way, that seemed a more likely candidate for Morgan's efforts. And I started to think that instead of the neighbour—

Natalie.

Instead of Natalie, maybe Morgan would go put his phone in his car overnight, so he wasn't tempted to use it in the house.

Beta mentioned she'd heard recently of another academic, a highly regarded scholar, also using fiction writing of some sort in combination with philosophical dialogues about technology.

We might even be able to invite her out for an event, she said.

That'd be great, I offered.

The ambivalent quality of my initial feelings suggested that I saw this scholar as both comrade and competition.

And I loved the crows! Continued Beta. *Clacking*. It's like your fingernails on glass.

Beta pulled her phone from her pocket and demonstrated with her nails. I pulled out my phone and did the same. We both laughed, a break in the discussion that I used as an opportunity to point to my cheek so as to alert Beta to the presence of the crumbs on her chin. She attempted to dislodged them with a disinterested flick but the crumbs still clung there.

So much more pleasing than our sonically impoverished swipes, said Beta, as she continued to rap her nails on the screen.

I actually fictionalised that bit in the story, I said. In real life the crows were two children. These young kids, a boy and a girl, who used to sneak through the hole in the fence, just as keen as the crows I described, and as you suggest, it was the sound their fingernails on the glass, that and their squeals of laughter, that would wake me up every morning.

5. Fairly defined gradations

In my first email exchanges with Jed about the project she wrote of metaphors for the soil, specifically the metaphors of 'soil as bucket' and 'soil as sponge' and the different conceptual implications of each. Bucket was commonly used by scientists and agronomists, whereas sponge was Jed's new alternative, and not commonly used. Bucket suggested a more static role played by soil as a vessel or container. Sponge, by contrast, implied that soil was active in soaking things up.

Jed wrote of her hopes to design a visualisation that connected with farmers.

They are very keen to create a metaphor, wrote Jed, or a visualisation that harmonises the farmer's mental models and understandings with the data and science.

When they see the visualisation, his email continued, I hope it accords with their intuitive and experiential understanding and validates their knowledge.

In my replies to Jed, I emphasised how much I liked the sponge metaphor and connected her idea to what, in hindsight, were quite fanciful references, such as the notion of porosity applied to urban space in the writing of a certain philosophically minded German writer, and the metaphor of foam, which, like a sponge, was similarly an air-filled material.

My next exchange with Jed was over the phone, maybe two or three months later. I was working from home at the time but walked outside to the small park near our house to make the call. Being on the phone made me want to move around and the apartment only allowed for limited explorations.

The park occupied a thin strip of land in-between two roads, protected by some relatively large figs and plane trees at the borders. There was a strangely popular children's playground in the middle of the park. My partner and I often speculated about why the playground was so well patronised. There were no conspicuous reasons. I'd made a mental note that I might one day talk to some of the park users to get to the bottom of things.

I tended to stay away from the playground and instead spent my time walking on the grassy strip between the plane trees at the other end.

I asked Jed about her sponge metaphor on the phone. Things seemed to have changed. Jed mentioned how when she began the project she imagined that her own poetic insights would form the basis for the best solution to the design problem. Jed came to realise however that the people who used her design were the more likely determinants of its success, and they seemed to want simple, clarified visuals.

Most of the maps Jed was designing depicted abstract or non-visible aspects of soil, like pH, so her charts tended to reflect this, rather than expressing the feeling or poetics of soil.

So I feel like there are two competing concerns, said Jed, my own ideas and interests and what the users want.

Despite this apparent tension, Jed was having a great time working on the project. The project team, the scientists, the agronomists and farmers were all insightful and friendly. Jed was enjoying the challenge and the encounter with new kinds of conceptual and practical knowledge.

We also talked about naming conventions for farm paddocks. Jed asked a question that provoked me to speculate about the different criteria used to identify paddocks on the farm where I grew up and where my parents and brother still lived and worked. The categories for paddocks included:

- the names of people, usually last names: Williamson's, Riley's, Halliday's, Woodhouse's

- manmade features or infrastructure, such as the Tin Hut, Williamson's Mill, The Dump Paddock, Tin Hut Tank Paddock, The House Paddock and Williamson's Yards

- paddock shapes: Riley's Long, Williamson's Long

- paddock locations: Bottom Stains, Top Stains, Middle Stains, Top Lucerne, Top Williamson's

- topographical features: Tin Hut Bumpy Paddock, The Red Creek

- vegetation features: Tin Hut Trees, Tin Hut Timber, Riley's Cultivation, Riley's Grass, Bottom Lucern, The Linseed Paddock

- paddocks named after the animals they often contained: The Horse Paddock, The Cow Paddock.

There didn't seem to be anything surprising about the list or the criteria on which they were based. I mentioned to Jed that I had wondered recently whether there were any farms that used radically different naming conventions and she said that one of the farmers she'd been working with had named a paddock after something that happened to a human in it: The Broken Leg Paddock.

The Epiphany Paddock, The Bad Thought Paddock, The Lost Pocket Knife Paddock, The Lost Mobile Phone Paddock, The Paddock Where

I Hid a Beer Bottle up in a Kurrajong Tree on New Years Eve While Plowing...

After our conversation, I returned to the apartment and continued to think about the paddocks at the farm and the soils in each of them. Initially I began listing the soil attributes, such as colour and consistency: Silo Stains has an orange-coloured soil that in my memory seemed bare and compact, relatively naked of the thicker organic matter evident in Bottom Stains, O'Donnell's and Woodhouse's.

While this was enjoyable in the short term I suspected it might soon become uninteresting, so I decided to set myself a challenge of the imagination: to compose fictional characters based on the qualities associated with soils in the different paddocks.

This too remained futile and unproductive as the only thing I could come up with was a balding, orange-haired boy with flaking skin called Silo Stains. Anything else I imagined about this character had little meaningful connection with the soil in the paddock.

After some testing of various mental exercises of this type, I decided the problem was in limiting myself to certain paddocks, rather than beginning with memories of the soil. If thinking about soil was the main purpose of the exercise, as it seemed to have become, then paddocks weren't the best orienting criteria; paddocks were the wrong kind of abstraction.

Freed from a paddock-oriented criteria, the first memories that came to mind were of digging, of being bogged or trying to avoid getting bogged, of picking up rocks, mainly limestone, and examining the worlds of critters revealed at the interface of above and below ground.

The next time I spoke with Jed was from one of picnic huts that I habitually used as an office at the beach. Jed wanted to show me some of her designs, so we spoke through the screens of our laptops.

I proudly swung my computer around to share the beachside outlook of my desk.

As in our previous discussions, Jed emphasised how her visualisations had for the most part taken on an abstract, schematic quality, guided by the pragmatics of use, rather than the poetics of soil. She talked me through her visualisations for determining soil water-holding capacity, soil pH, soil texture and soil carbon, and showed me maps of paddocks where such information was displayed from an aerial perspective. Curved boundaries and blob-like shapes demarcated brightly coloured areas corresponding to soil qualities based on specific measurements. The areas were defined by firm and clear borders—between green and yellow, for example—a design decision that Jed explained was based how the maps would be used: a blended or diffuse blurring of green into yellow might capture some of the ambiguity in the way soil characteristics were distributed across a given area, but in the end farmers and agronomists would be required to act as though there was a clear border. There wasn't much point in having the visualisations if they simply delegated the burden of such decision making and interpretation back onto human users at inopportune times.

When Jed used the phrase 'management zones' to describe her maps, I took this as an opportunity to share some thoughts I had about the arbitrariness of fence-lines as borders for determining the way paddocks were managed. Paddocks were in essence management zones, but their placement and shape often had little to do with soil and the complexities of landscape ecology. On grazing properties, fences were typically built to control the flow of animals into and out of paddocks. While the size and shape of paddocks varied based on approaches to livestock management—cell grazing, for example, required smaller paddocks and more frequent stock rotations—the underlying paddock configuration was often determined by borders associated with often redundant histories of landownership and the conveniences of topography.

I wondered the extent to which my dad and brother would change the placement and size of our paddocks, if given free labour and expenses for a new configuration, and whether different criteria, such as soil characteristics, might be taken into consideration. A question for a future discussion with them, no doubt.

Jed also mentioned a list of farm features she was creating to help users orient themselves in her visualisations and to provide additional information about a farm. In Geographic Information Systems (GIS) such features can be specified as points, lines or areas. Her areas included: residences, sheds, dams and conservation management areas. Lines included: rivers, routes and fences. Points included: windmills, trees, tanks and troughs. I asked why a dam was an area and not a point, since a small dam and a large tank could be close to the same size. Jed said that although in reality nothing is a single point, when zooming in or out on a GIS map, the areas and lines get bigger or smaller, whereas the symbols for points remain the same size. Perhaps, said Jed, tanks, like dams, needed to be areas. I saw her making a note with her pen in a sketch pad on the desk next to the computer.

The next time I spoke to Jed I was at the kitchen table back at the family farm. We'd arranged a discussion over video conference with my dad and brother, Brett, in response to the visual language Jed was developing for soil and land management.

Dad was having a piece of cake and tea after his lunch and I made my brother a mint tea, as he was on one of his fasting days and didn't intend to eat until dinner. I put my smartphone on the table to record the conversation and arranged a chair for dad and Brett facing the laptop. Then I squeezed between the backs of the chairs and the wall so I could see Jed on the screen too.

Can I ask, said Dad, the technology, is it satellite technology? Are you walking over the ground with ECG? Or is it actually taking soil samples?

Good question, said Jed, and she proceeded to explain how the digital tool she was developing used publicly available data, like gamma radiometrics, that could in turn be used to make a predictions about the best spots to do soil samples, rather than having to collect samples at a much greater and therefore more time- and cost-intensive scale.

OK, said Brett.

Right, said dad.

Jed mentioned that what interested her in the project as a designer was the challenge of how to best show the data, and then how to consider the perspective of users and adapt the visualisations to their perspectives.

Right, said Brett.

OK, said dad.

Jed added that soil maps are great from far away but when you zoom in at the farm level, it's all one single colour, because the resolution is just too big.

One of the good features of this tool, said Jed, is that it goes down to ten metres resolution across the paddock and, I think, increments as far down as 1 cm.

Right, said Brett.

What I was going to ask you guys for some feedback on, said Jed, was your take on the work so far, if there's anything that jumps out at you as seeming a bit weird or doesn't fit your expectation of what you thought you'd see, or if something is working well...

Happy to, said dad.

Very happy to, said Brett.

Jed shared her different visualisations of soil attributes and explained the rationale informing her design decisions. Dad and Brett offered terse but seemingly helpful replies that I watched Jed write down in her notebook.

They're good, Dad would say, in response to one of Jed's visuals, or *that's intuitive*. Brett commented that in one instance he found the labels a more intuitive guide to reading the image than the colours, which Jed duly noted. Dad pointed out that straight rather than curved lines would be more appropriate.

In some cases dad would begin to tell stories about the geography and soil types based on the visualisations, positioning the otherwise contextless images in a place and imagining his own farm in relation to it. The images provoked dad to travel through a virtual space in his mind and take Jed on his journey.

Jed showed an image that depicted vertical gradations of acid levels in the soil.

Your numbers are upside-down, said Dad. We're more acidic on the surface than down below. You must be up on the Liverpool Plains.

Dad also contrasted the digital images and the possibility of a digital system with the so-called 'deep litter system' of his desk, where the transects for his farm were reportedly buried.

At times the discussion hinted at submerged philosophical questions that were mixed in with more pragmatic talk. Jed described her now discarded approach to visualisation that depicted the transition between soil types as blended, rather than in distinct bands.

Our actions are discrete or finite anyway, said Dad, so we need to have some place where to draw the line. Levels in fairly defined gradations, so if you have a border, that's much more helpful to make decisions.

I listened carefully to the exchange, both in the room with Brett and Dad, squeezed behind the two chairs at our kitchen table, and then later, in Sydney, listening to the recording on my phone on runs around the park with my earphones in.

As I listened I wondered about the peculiarities of this particular exchange and how it differed from other kinds of exchange; the great panoply of verbal exchanges that compose our ordinary lives, whether of formal or informal varieties, in different practical contexts: confessions, heart-to-hearts, discussions about favourite things, promises, inaugurations, evaluations, critiques, orders, complaints, greetings and salutations and the offering of street directions plus many more besides.

The participants in this particular dialogue were engaged in thinking about the nature of the artificial. The conversation involved the evocation and refinement of a still-mutable, hypothetical entity, brought to life by images and specifications for how it might be used in particular contexts. The discussion was oriented towards the future, requiring the speakers to imagine something not yet familiar. Although the evolving dialogue also drew on the tacit, cumulative, existing knowledges of Brett and Dad, who told Jed when and how they thought the visualisations would be useful.

One moment especially stood out as encapsulating the broader possibilities of such genres of conversation. Jed was describing a map that might depict changes in nitrogen levels in the soil over time—or any other measurable soil attribute for that matter—like a weather or pressure map with dynamic depictions of phenomena over a given period.

It would be interesting to document that for carbon over a ten-year period, said Brett, how the carbon content of your soil changes, how it's influenced by seasons and longer term trends...

It'd be fascinating to see, agreed Dad, and you don't quite know how you would respond to that piece of information...but it would be fascinating to see that in a visual format, I must say...

***

Some months later, on a return visit to the farm, I witnessed Brett transformed by the knowledge of soil he'd recently learned. He motioned with his hands to show how the body of the soil expands and contracts. He'd recently finished a soil science graduate certificate and I envisaged his new knowledge as a causal force pulsing through his mind and body, expanding and contracting like the soil he gesturally described. Brett was taking me out on a tour of the paddocks so he could better articulate his knowledge by pointing to and touching the soil.

Water changes the form of the soil, said Brett, and soil is distinguished by the extent to which it undergoes such changes. Here in this paddock, in this location, it expands and contracts quite a lot. Up in North West NSW, there are places where the soil shrinks and expands so much you get big dams forming in the ground. They can't build on there because the soil moves so much. Clay, when it gets wet, it expands.

But we weren't standing in North West NSW, we were in the Central West, on Wiradjuri land.

Brett and Dad had recently dug a silage pit, which was the first location for my tour. The recent drought and climate change had them thinking ahead, banking grass in the ground for the future. Incidentally, the intrusion into the soil created a display so sorts: walls of soil rising up as the ground is lowered through the removal of soil.

We stood in the pit while we talked. Brett pointed to the soil, the wall, the black surface.

It's unusual, said Brett. We have this black soil here and the valley in O'Donnell's. He pointed down the slope of a gully to the north-east. And in a few more places...in The Tin Hut.

Brett said that soils stratified naturally over time and that Australian soils are quite old, so they demonstrate this stratification.

They've got this layer of organic matter, said Brett, and as you go down it gets higher in clay. It changes colour. You can see, it's a yellow colour here, then it changes to brown.

This soil is unusual, Brett repeated, it's got a really high pH. Most of the soils around here are quite acidic. Can you see these things here?

It's like lime, I said. Like the gravel in the driveway.

It's calcium, said Brett, that has re-formed. So, when the acidity of the soil increases, which happens in farming systems, then hydrogen ions will react with this calcium, and it buffers the soil. So there is no chance of this soil becoming too acidic.

Because of the calcium? I asked.

Because of the amount of calcium, said Brett. Unless there is so much acid that it will dissolve all of the calcium we can see here. Like acid rain or something.

I conceptualised my job, my research aim, as describing the character of this *event*: the arrival of soil science onto a farm. For a while I had imagined my task as describing a *being*: storytellers have given form to gods, to humans, to monsters, demons and other creatures—*what then, is the being or creature of knowledge, how can I animate it in words?* Should I be describing a parasitical form that is spread much like a virus and then inhabits and grows in particular ecological contexts where humans are typically present? But as soon as I drift towards being, to character, I'm struck by the inadequacy of analogy, of steady, readymade morphisms, whether zoomorphism, anthropomorphism or technomorphism. No, my job is to trace the path of a *vector* in an *event*, as it pulses through a cascading series of transformations to which I bear witness; the knowledge that animates the brain and the body of Brett on his farm.

I recalled a shadow impression of Brett's hands and the space between them: smaller, then bigger; expanding and contracting.

It's called black or brown vertisol soil, said Brett, picking up some of the darker soil in his hand. The clay structure is such that it absorbs water and then it shrinks and expands. And that's why it forms this fine crumb.

This is not caused by sheep, continued Brett. It has shrunk and expanded and shrunk and expanded. You see it crack and it just erodes away. Not great for the silage pit. But very fertile and good for seeding. It's really fine. Best soil we've got anywhere in the place, often it's found on alluvial planes, in a gully, a wash area, like this. It must go all the way down the gully I think. It's not on the other side... you can see the road there. It's only here. It might even stop below that big dam.

I asked Brett why the soil is so fertile.

High cation exchange capacity, said Brett. Means lots of plant-available nutrients. Come over this side, it's quite cool.

We walked over to the other side of the pit.

It has these kinds of waves in the soil from the shrinking and expanding of the clay. According to Brett, Dad didn't even know.

We knew it was good, dark soil here, said Brett, but in terms of knowing...if we had known we probably wouldn't have put the silage pit here. Its prone to erosion now and we made quite a steep bank...you can see it's already getting little gullies down it. The ideal soil would be the type of clay that they make bricks from, which doesn't expand at all. Kaolinite or something...they are generally low-quality soils.

We drove in the ute to another paddock, to the Tin Hut Bumpy Paddock. I asked Brett whether his new knowledge had changed the way he manages things.

Don't know if it has changed much, he said, after a long pause.

It changes the way you think, continued Brett, it gives you tools to think differently about something...when you can identify it you're more engaged with it I suppose, but you're not necessarily doing anything differently, I don't think...Yeah, we're not doing anything particularly different but we're probably more aware, if something did become a problem, like the soil acidity, I'd be in a better position to know what to do and what's causing it.

Brett and I occupied a patch of earth, the distance between us was small enough to converse and exchange objects. Brett hammered a probe into the ground, a homemade soil probe constructed from cut pipe. The rhythmic, ominous sound of steel on steel filled the landscape. The probe cut deep into the ground. Our force and desire to know was telescoped downwards, the sound, however, radiated out, dispersing through the landscape, locating our activity in an inverse motion.

The probe was so tight in the ground that Brett had to hammer it out, hammer upwards so the tool rose. The probe contained soil, visible through the strip of steel Brett had removed from the side of the pipe. Before, the soil was too hard to remove from the pipe because the gap

91

was too narrow; now, according to Brett, it's too wide, some of the soil towards the top had fallen out.

But it'll do, said Brett.

Brett scattered a fine white powder on the soil, barium sulphate. The powder turned green.

Pretty ideal, that is, he said, pretty ideal.

I imagined the walls of the small cavity, like a hyper-condensed version of the silage pit, marked with waves of stratified soil. Brett had mentioned the surprising porosity of the soil, air in the ground, fifty percent porosity, as much air as life and rock; space folded so intricately as to give the impression of hardness. Removing the earth, making it crudely legible, released my mind into such depths, the intricate pores that marked the earth, the fine networks that gave form to the impenetrable architecture beneath us.

6. The customers

I was to accompany a group of design researchers working for a large multinational corporation on a research trip to a remote, regional community. The purpose of the trip, from the perspective of the researchers, was to uncover insights about how people in the community used and felt about kitchen utensils. It was exploratory research. One of my colleagues had told a friend at the company that she worked with a design academic who used to be a poet and now published literary fiction. This news reached the corporation's head of the design, who suggested that I shadow his research team on one of their field trips. He thought that I might be able to describe what the team did in a distinctive and engaging way. According to the head of design, his profession suffered from troubles with language, particularly within those areas of design that involved researching people rather than making things.

This particular trip involved local residents taking the research team on a tour through one of the new medium-density housing development on the outskirts of their growing rural town. There must have been a body of water nearby that the locals used for recreation, a river or a dam, as many of the houses had boats and jetskis parked out the front on trailers attached to sizable utility vehicles. Many of the houses had either small or large barking dogs and impeccably mown oblongs of lawn. It was a very bright day.

The four members of the research team, Selvina, Delta, Jont and Clay, gave off a certain effervescent, forced friendliness that I assumed had been forged on similar trips, perhaps in circumstances of greater adversity. The research team called people *customers*, since this feature of their being was of primary importance for the purposes of the research. From the perspective of the so-called customers, I was just another member of the research team. I'm not sure how much the customers were being paid for participating, but I suspected they must have been compensated in some way on account of their general enthusiasm.

From what I could gather, the research was intended to give the company a better understanding of the people who used its service by obtaining knowledge about the objects they had in their houses, how they used these objects and the values the customers attached to them. Many other details about the research remained obscure, though there seemed to be a particular focus on kitchen appliances and accessories.

I was reminded a little of the window-washing job I did during university, washing both the outside and inside of windows in usually quite large houses with abundant glass; going from house to house around the city and forming vague and fanciful accounts of the lives lived by the people in these dwellings based on fragmentary impressions gleaned from family photos, notes stuck to fridges, peeks at pantry contents and any sense of character that emerged through an overall aesthetic or hints of a lifestyle.However, when I felt uncomfortable on those occasions it was on account of being an intruder, who was meant to work invisibly and whose success was to some extent contingent on not making my presence felt. On the field trip, I felt uncomfortable due to a sense I was making the occupants feel strange within their own homes. There was also little chance for the more gentle, incidental speculation that came on window-washing jobs, when I worked in largely undisturbed silence. On the field trip, by contrast, any speculative story that started to emerge in my imagination was quickly snuffed by a direct interaction between one of the research team and a customer.

We stopped regularly on our shuffles through the different rooms in new, often sharply fragranced houses and listened to a customers discuss objects and aspects of the spaces in which they lived. Sometimes members of the team would speak up after a customer had finished a story, either to ask for clarification or affirm what they thought was right.

Over time, the tone of voice and the content of the interjections began to give colour to different researchers in the team. Selvina was often keen to know what people called the different appliances. When Selvina's inquiries were not satisfied she exerted her own knowledge and in these moments it was unclear whether the customers were educating the research team or the research team were educating the customers.

On one occasion Selvina asked a customer to repeat a story about a particular cooking utensil. When the customer's reply did not suffice, Selvina began to direct the conversation with questions that soon started to sound like statements of fact.

You prefer the stove top for coffee, don't you?

Delta chimed in with an anecdote about the customers at another dwelling, who preferred a plunger—as though this were a rare bit of trivia.

Some members of the research team already knew quite a bit about customers and their everyday lives. These members were keen to share this knowledge, both with the team and with the customers, particularly when the customers seemed a little reticent or unsure.

The practice of coffee-drinking was an enduring curiosity for the group and when one customer pointed to numerous appliances in cupboards and on the benchtop, a series of questions about the practice followed from various members of the team.

The customer was asked whether his family prefers to drink out of ceramic, glass, plastic or paper.

Selvina noted that even though she rarely drinks coffee, in her opinion ceramic is by far the best option.

Paper cups and plastic are not sustainable options, said Selvina, which seemed to imply that the customers might be at fault.

We paused by the fridge in the third house we visited, and a customer recounted a story about how whenever he returned to his childhood home, checking the fridge would be among the first things he would do, as though the bounty stored inside would be the primary determinant of his mood for a certain length of time.

The customer told us that the plastic drawer at the bottom of the fridge was called a 'crisper' on account of the attribute of crispness, which his family valued greatly in both fruit and vegetables.

Selvina asked the customer the 'real' name of the crisper and he hesitantly suggested that it might simply be called a fridge drawer.

It's made from Perspex, said Selvina, and the customer conceded that it may indeed be made from Perspex.

What would you say this helps you to accomplish? was another question asked by the team. *How frequently do you use it? What other things do you use it with? When do you use it?*

The 'creature comforts' that customers appeared to value was a favourite topic of conversation. I have mentioned coffee. Alcohol, too, was another substance with which the customers seemed to have an intimate relationship. An ambivalent consensus emerged within the team: some customers desired alcohol when they were shown certain images.

One group member, Clay, noted that he spoke to a customer who had given up alcohol because of other medication, and reported that this customer claimed not to really miss it anyway, except when going out to dinner with friends.

They claim food and wine go together, said Clay, and cola or juice are not suitable substitutes.

A whisky, too, added Selvia, at the end of a day of work. This is something that some customers appear to enjoy.

The research team sniggered at this idea.

For my part, I was bothered during the trip by not having my usual access to the supply of delectable sugary pastries and cakes that I routinely consumed throughout the day. These artful combinations of sugar, fat, carbohydrate and caffeine were evidently more crucial to my emotional stability than I'd previously imagined. I enjoyed initiating conversations with members of the research team about the different treats I liked, as though in allegiance to the customers they studied.

The customers were often asked to repeat the *real* use of the different things they described. When a customer described the way different implements in a drawer were used, Selvina questioned her about why she bought so many implements for essentially the same task.

When confronted with these questions, the customer looked searchingly at the wall of the house, as though it depicted a horizon to another distant landscape. The customer could do no better than speculate that she didn't always act in perfectly rational ways. She was prey to the forces of creativity that circulated in an unstable fashion and which on occasion found expression in items or tools that members of the research might regard as frivolous.

Waste became a topic of conversation in the strange atmosphere of a customer's garage. A discussion erupted about how some things, once in the possession of the customers, seemed to devalue over time, while others became more valuable. Some members of the research team were surprised to hear from a customer that she would adapt, appropriate and personalise certain objects over time, while other objects she attempted to keep in the same condition permanently.

Some customers had techniques for deflecting the inquiries of the researchers. One customer would often say both 'yeah' and 'nah' in quick succession, before moving on to the next topic of conversation. Often customers expressed bemusement because certain details seemed so important to the group, as though the research team were besotted by phenomena that, for the customer, didn't matter at all. But in general, the customers responded to the questions in good humour.

One customer told a story about her ring, which featured an opaque white stone that was elliptical in form and mounted in gold. She had designed it with her mother.

We admired the ring while she talked. She wore the ring all the time, she said.

She added that the ring had become part of her image, and she feared that if she were to lose the ring she might damage this image, which gave coherence and distinctiveness to her concept of self.

If you get in the habit of regularly putting it on and taking it off, said Selvina, you will indeed be more likely to lose it.

Delta then told a story about a treasured object she had lost. On this occasion, the object was a necklace. Like the ring, it was also a family heirloom that represented a special connection between daughter and mother. Delta left the necklace at a particular location and couldn't find it when she went back to look. She was not, Delta claimed, usually the kind of person who lost things.

Delta worried her mother would be angry at her for losing the necklace. She had only lost three other things in her life: a bag and two jackets. The bag, she lost at a festival while getting a massage. Delta returned to the same festival the next year with a vision that the jacket might still be there on the ground, where she'd got the massage. The two jackets had also been lost at festivals, one by her friend.

The research team agreed that lost objects seem to stay with a person, often vividly in their memories, sometimes more so than the objects they still possessed.

At the conclusion of the day the research team offered a series of performances to show their gratitude for the efforts of customers. Over the course of the trip the team had started to playfully repeat the names customers used to identify objects, images, practices and spaces.

Selvina stipulated that the performance had to involve the whole team, which included me. We all stood. Selivina had given us each four names to chant. My names were for non-electronic implements: *cheese grater, cutting board, whisk, wok.*

I shared my hesitations about the performance with Delta, who I anticipated would be sympathetic. We were both anxious about how the performance would be received by the customers but Delta suggested my self-consciousness wouldn't necessarily be an accurate indication of what the customers felt.

We gathered on the outdoor deck of one of the houses, with a small crowd of customers that we'd visited over the day. We hadn't rehearsed our performance. Most of the time the names were chanted out of time, or too quietly to be heard. Sometimes the names were mispronounced. Selvina was the conductor and moved around directing which of us to chant. The customers laughed heartily and shared glances with each other.

Back in the city I spoke with Clay and Delta about the trip. I had been invited to the presentations the teams within the company had been asked to give about their research. They asked whether the trip was what I expected. I found the question hard to answer.

Clay asked whether I'd seen the grater one of the customers had given Selvina. Clay described the customer who gave the gift. I remembered seeing this customer standing some distance away from the group. The customer, to my knowledge, didn't utter a word for the duration of our visit. Delta and Clay both informed me, however, that Selvina had struck up a conversation with the customer and they talked a great deal. According to Clay, when we said goodbye after the performance the customer had quietly presented the grater to Selvina.

It was a beautiful grater, made from steel, quite small compared to others I'd seen, said Clay. Although Selvina wore glasses, and it was hard to see her eyes, it was clear she was very emotional receiving this gift.

Back at my apartment, collecting the light of the early morning in my eyes, I found myself repeating the four names I had chanted for the customers: *cheese grater, cutting board, whisk, wok. Cheese grater, cutting board, whisk, wok...*

7. The gully

Something about it isn't right, apparently. No, she liked that. No, the face was fine. No, she actually liked that. Yep. Yep. All those bits. No. The conversation, the voice. I don't know. Yes. Yes. A bit stumped. But it depends. It depends. It depends, Tracey. On what she means by possibility. I don't know either. Yes. Yes. Yes, in the end it might not be. No, it never is. We have to make her think it is. I don't care. No, I know you don't either. Sorry. Sorry. Yes, we've been here before, annoying that it doesn't make it any easier. I'll go back to the storyboards. I agree, I think the sound is as important. Who knows what else. Who knows. Maybe we need to drug her beforehand. Seriously. Hahaha. Hahahaha. OK. OK.

I enjoyed writing down their phone conversations. Dialogues heard as soliloquies. I shifted between imagining the life of the speaker on the other end of the line or focusing exclusively on their words, as though the language were a poem in its own right. I started trying to replicate my own 'phone conversation poems' in parallel, based on these conventions.

Dennis and Tracey were two tutors at the university who spent most of their time running a small business that created immersive narrative experiences. These could be installations in galleries or at creative media events, one-off pieces for businesses attempting to communicate abstract ideas in relatable ways, or sometimes events for wealthy individuals. I often heard them talking in the shared workspace and due to our shared interest in narrative, we struck up a working relationship. Our approach and aims were pretty loose: I'd listen to their conversations and write about them, where possible offering them conceptual and editorial feedback on the narrative aspects of their projects.

Not long into our relationship, Dennis and Tracey started working for a client who they'd initially described as a dream come true: someone with a lot of money who had a relatively open brief. Nothing was out of scope.

I hadn't met the client, Alex, nor was I present at the inception meeting. However, she was a big reader, and seemed to take an interest in design history, which was why Dennis and Tracey engaged me in the project more directly than they typically might.

Alex wanted to recreate a particular encounter of personal significance. Her vision filtered down to me through Dennis and Tracey's discussions and the prototypes for the experience they were building at work—one of the advantages, they said, of being tutors at university was that you could use the facilities for projects like this, up to a point.

Alex had a particular memory that visited her at random moments. It irrigated her life—Dennis emphasised that 'irrigated' was Alex's word. When this memory returned to her at random, it was far more pleasurable than when she sought it out deliberately. Though she still sought it out deliberately, and it still gave her pleasure when she did, it wasn't, in Alex's words, a benchmark experience.

The memory involved a week staying at a house on a lake with a group of friends. Alex had been much younger, in her early twenties. She'd gone for a walk down to the edge of the lake to enjoy the twilight after having a couple of drinks. She sat on the bank for a while and then went for a swim. On her way back to the house Alex met one of the other house guests who she didn't know very well. They stopped and talked for a while, Alex still dripping from the swim and holding her clothes. She walked back to the house and enjoyed the warmth of the encounter and the sense of possibility it brought to her life.

That was it. On the surface it might not sound particularly complicated, at least not in terms of the plot. But as Dennis and Tracey soon discovered, the more they worked to recreate the idea, the more complex it became and the boundless scope of the brief started to cause problems.

For example, Alex was obsessed about the consistency of her skin after the swim. It felt dry, less supple than usual. However, it was a particular kind of dryness. Not, apparently, the uncomfortable sort.

Dennis and Tracey's 'media agnostic' approach led to all kinds of ideas for recreating this particular quality demanded by Alex. They seriously considered building a dam on the land Alex had said they could use to recreate her experience. Users—primarily Alex, but also the guests who she wished to share in her memories—would be led through a sequence of exercises to prepare their sensorium for reliable bliss.

Do whatever you like to it, she said, fill the whole thing with milk, I don't care. Just make it work.

The conundrum they soon faced boiled down to a question of abstraction. Was a more or less literal recreation of the events Alex described the best way to induce the feelings she craved, or, by contrast, should they attempt to isolate and recreate particular qualities—like her dry but not uncomfortably dry skin? And, relatedly: to what extent was her benchmark experience contingent on randomness? And how could they design the requisite randomness into their experience? Did Alex want her guests to share in her enjoyment, or experience their own kind of suggestively related, meaningful memory?

God, I don't know Dennis. It's impossible. No we're not doing that. I wasn't serious. Yes. Yes. Yes. Yes. Yep. You can't even tell. Can't even tell if it's there. You just can't. Well what's the point. Don't give me that shit about absence again. Well you heard her. If that's the best we've got you better be a good sell. You'll need to do even better. I wouldn't know where to start. It's probably not even legal. I'm tempted to just go back to the headset. Well, you know what they say about the perfect. I agree. No, I agree. I totally agree with that but not with the implications...

At a certain point in the project a consensus emerged between Dennis and Tracey that they'd been focusing on the wrong thing. In short, they decided that they hadn't accounted enough for Alex, specifically, and what they'd started calling 'the human percipient', in their efforts to recreate a moment of sublime reverie.

It took multi-hour sessions every day for more than a week to arrive at this consensus. A common characteristic of such sessions was the seeming feeling of utter creative exhaustion. Each time, Tracey and Dennis would reach a point in their brainstorming where the volume of good or even decent ideas seemed to dry up and they'd be left with a bad version of an idea they had earlier in the session or a hastily proposed new idea that, in its lack of coherence, distinctiveness and feasibility, could barely be called an idea at all.

Dennis, in particular, would look at me with bloodshot eyes, tapping the table between us with his finger as though the gesture might inflate a sense of shared conviction in the room. After these sessions, they'd both make surly departures and return to the specifics of their individual creative efforts. In Tracey's case, this was building a 3D virtual environment that contained exactly the right mix of overt and obscure visual stimulus to induce in Alex's imagination the act of remembering, while Dennis would return to his increasingly elaborate, hand-drawn landscape designs. The overall conception of the project was contingent on finding a way for these two artificial places to meet in a complimentary manner. The wheels typically fell off when either fell into the trap of imagining the other as secondary.

The idea to 'focus more on Alex rather than the thing' had the advantage of avoiding some of these seemingly inevitable creative tensions. It became less about the digital versus the landscape, and more about what they started calling 'imaginative fertility'—initially, it was 'imaginative facility' but Dennis misheard and they decided the error was more agreeable.

Dennis and Tracey didn't seem to be motivated by a reactive move away from technique and technology. If anything the opposite was true. They realised they needed to come up with an even more nuanced program, albeit not the kind of 'program' they'd initially imagined. Instead of placing all of their emphasis on the immediate encounter between Alex and the experience they designed, they decided to focus on a longer timespan, which included the 'consistency' of the human percipient—'consistency' was another word that I initially found esoteric when applied to humans. Tracey liked to use it a lot.

We need to prepare the user, Tracey would say. We need to ensure they are the right consistency.

For this, they enlisted me.

Do you mind…this is going to sound weird but just run with it. Do you mind listening to me while I tell you about an idea, but don't just listen passively, or don't just give the appearance you're listening passively, interrupt me so I have to clarify things further, so that than it introduces apparent discontinuity into my speech. Yeah. No. It's for this project. It's hard to explain. I think it's just best if we focus on the specifics of what I've just explained. OK. Does that make sense? OK. Yeah, that's right, I've got to go meet her. She's a director. You'll know some of the ads. That's right. That's what makes it hard. Look her up. Look her up. Hahahahaha. Yes, on Friday. On Friday. No that's always been the date. Do you mind if I call you back now and I'll just begin with a short hello and then start telling you the idea.

This is just some of the kind of zany stuff we do, Dennis had said to Alex when suggesting that they'd be sending her a real live novelist, who, what's more, wrote a bit about design.

I started writing a story as soon as I knew Alex's address. It began with me sitting at a computer looking at her house in the gully behind the beach, first from an aerial view, and then from street view, which in this case didn't reveal much.

I imagined asking Alex to tell me about her house over the phone while I looked at it from above. I imagined her in a chair wearing jeans and a white t-shirt. Her hair was still wet from the shower and when she spoke she twirled it between her fingers.

From above, the house look as though it had an ample front lawn. A red-gravel driveway curved in an almost complete circle on the other side of the house, a large tree, perhaps a fig, stretched out in fractal form at its centre. I imagined my arrival: walking over the lawn on the gully side in the fading light of the day and the sound of insects rising ahead of me into the darkness.

I looked Alex up online. She had a reasonably distinctive last name so most of the images on the search were indirectly or directly related to her, however there were a few stray images: construction site equipment and a man eating sandwich of some sort in the background; a YouTube still of a bearded man facing the camera, with a hat and a plastic model laid out on the table in front of him; a pile of bright leather bands; and a group of kids on a novelty train ride. Setting aside these anomalies, I learnt that Alex had been an actress for a brief while, then a creative producer, and now a director who also owned her own production studio.

I became particularly fascinated by one image where Alex held a small, black cat in one hand and a cigarette in the other. There was a glass of red wine in the foreground on the righthand side and a cigarette lighter on the table. Alex appeared to be talking to the cat, her lips were open and her mouth was slightly off-kilter, one lip edging downward, slightly lower than the other. There was a dark, patterned curtain in the background, a white wall and a poster half obscured by Alex's bare shoulder.

As I walked up the gully towards Alex's house, I tried to piece together the dream I'd had the previous night. Alex had come to visit my family home. She was someone I wanted to impress. We shared a history together, not specified in the dream, and had I hoped to find some photos to show her that recorded this time. Although these photos would typically be valuable for the nostalgic emotions they induced, in this context it was clear Alex was going to evaluate them based on aesthetic criteria, as though the quality of personal significance and the quality of a more generalised beauty were the same thing. I couldn't find any photos, so instead she just looked through other photos I'd taken during the same period, which didn't include her. She sat on the couch with her feet up on the cushions and while I watched her I was filled with disappointment that she couldn't look upon herself in the images and thereby confirm we had shared certain experiences.

In the next part of the dream, Alex had left my family home and I searched through the drawers in the wardrobe of my old bedroom looking for the photos that showed us together. Eventually, I found the photos and was filled with mixed feelings of joyous satisfaction on the one hand, as though I'd discovered some long lost treasure, and disappointment, on the other hand, as Alex had now departed and there was no opportunity to immediately share the images.

Of the photographs that showed us together, only the faintest impression remained in my memory, and now, as I looked into the dusty-green, crisscrossing branches of the lower-storey vegetation in the gully, I suspected that my present perception was in part warping the background of the image I'd dreamt and was now trying to recollect.

The central path followed a small stream that led along the length of the gully until it reached a set of stairs at the western end. I'd walked up the gully before but hadn't noticed how many different paths broke off from the central trail. The bare dirt of these little digressions was visible for a brief while before it disappeared in the vegetation that thickened on the slopes. I could occasionally hear a human voice in the distance, though I couldn't see any of the houses that surrounded the edges of the gully on the higher parts of the slope.

It would have been far easier to find Alex's house had I approached it from the street, however, I was committed on the more atmospheric entrance. Whether this was out of fidelity to my previous imaginings or due to some aesthetic ideal was difficult for me to say. As I walked, I observed elements of my surrounds that I imagined would be good to put in the story and decided to make audio notes of these on my phone. As I spoke, I felt compelled to formulate connective parts in-between each discrete observation, so rather than sounding like a list, my recording flowed in sentences, albeit with frequent long pauses while I gathered my thoughts to ensure continuity:

As I walked up the gully I wondered...how many different ways there might have been to describe such branches...and whether futility was the appropriate response...in the face of all the descriptions having been used many times before...The air got cooler as I walked up the gully...and occasionally the sound of a bird reminded me of a bush environment from my youth...The stairs at the end veered to the left...and away from a small waterfall below...spilling down...over multiple rock platforms...feeding the little creek...

Once higher...the path zagged back to the right, crossing the top of the creek...then rising again, to a dirt track...that traversed the top edge of the gully and gave...a gallery-like view...over the grasses in the foreground, to the canopy below…and the pale houses embedded in the green…slope on other side.

Both the gate into the drive of Alex's house and the front door were open when I arrived. The gravel driveway was smaller than I imagined and the gravel a darker, stronger red. I enjoyed the crunch of my steps announcing my arrival. In fact, the garden as a whole seemed smaller than I'd imagined, fractionally rather than dramatically, which had the effect of making it seem more delicate too. The tree I'd imagined was a fig was actually a magnolia and some of its soft petals lay scattered on the ground. The effect was decorative rather than messy. The house was old, at least one hundred years to my eye, and its style was picturesque, a touch whimsical, though not at all twee. The once-bright reds and blues had faded and the wood was washed of its colour, looking suitably like the pieces of sun- and salt-bleached driftwood that occasionally washed up at the beach.

The mood inside was markedly different. My first impression registered a recently designed space that looked and even smelt unlived in. There were scent sticks in vases disseminating a sickly sweet smell and prints of botanical drawings on the wall. The wallpaper was also patterned with botanicals: twisting green vines with large, perforated leaves and white and yellow flowers, some in profile and some in frontal view. In the absence of anything but an abstract and amorphous sense of her character, my feelings towards Alex as a person changed in tandem with my feelings towards the space and the assumed thinking behind it.

I could tell there was a candle alight in the next room so I called out to Alex and she appeared, with alarming speed, in the doorway between the rooms, greeting me with the wide, devilish smile that characterised her face in the images I'd seen online.

Great, she said, you've come, and she took my hand, repeating her initial salutation in a deeper, more gravelly voice.

I followed Alex into the next room, which featured two large, off-white couches and matched the mood of the previous room. As too did Alex's outfit, a billowing kaftan, almost see-through, patterned with flowing vines and large flowers. She gestured for me to sit on the couch adjacent to hers and proceeded to pour me a large glass of iced water.

After we exchanged a few questions about my work with Dennis and Tracey, I asked Alex whether she minded if I began our chat by playing the recording I'd made while walking through the gully to her house.

Of course, she said, waving her hand. She watched as I placed my phone down on the glass table between the couches and searched for the audio file in my archive of voice memos. Alex, seeing some of the other titles among the voice files, asked about '1950s house', which I'd recorded some months ago talking with my mother in the kitchen of house where I'd grown up.

Can we listen to it first? she said. I've just been reading about 1950s interiors.

I hesitantly agreed to this request, providing contextual detail about how I'd asked Mum if she had any memories of 1950s interiors during her childhood. I wanted to use these details as indirect references points for a book I was working on.

I pressed play, sat back in the couch, and my mother's voice started to fill the room.

'....pretty well broken into very basic units, you had a sink, a couple of cupboards and you had a work surface somewhere. In the new exhibition village, all the kitchens tried to customise particular ways of working in the kitchen, so they had things like a flour bin, they had specialised drawers that were dedicated to the storage of different dry ingredients. They also had features like pull-out cutting boards. See, that's the drawer front, and you'd pull that out like this. It was here...'

Alex looked at me intently while we listened. She reached behind the back of her couch to produce a small, opaque vessel with a screw lid, which revealed a white, pearly cream that she started to apply to her face in small dabs. She continued to rub it in while she looked away, so I could see her face in profile, and it appeared as though something had started to pain her a little. She closed her eyes and we both continued to listen.

"...that was part of the change I suppose...they tried to smarten them up, they made really nice edges on things...the kitchen became more than just a utility area, that changed, so you know, everything matched all the way around the room and went together, the sink became integrated into the bench, storage...rather than having jars and containers, they were integrated into the kitchen. They're the main kind of things..."

This is just fabulous, said Alex, and I wasn't sure whether she was talking about the recording or her cream.

Do you mind? she asked, and dipped two fingers into her pot, holding the cream-covered tips towards me in a little salute, which seemed to make the next phase of our interaction inevitable.

Alex climbed onto the couch beside me and pushed my fringe to the side of my face with one hand and began to spread the cream over my forehead with the other.

You'll look much more fuckable after this, she said.

She looked at my face intently, while I sat there in a mild, but not altogether unpleasant, state of shock.

The cream brought immediate relief to my skin, which I initially experienced as coolness rather than moisture, though soon I started feel a newfound suppleness that I gauged by opening my jaw wide.

My mother's voice continued to play in the background as Alex's fingers pressed into my skin with increasing firmness and speed.

'I think Laminex became a product of that era too, instead of wood I suppose, but my grandmother's sink, a 1920s sink, was porcelain. Umm...yeah...I only vaguely remember the kitchen from before we went to Perth...So you go into the next room, you go into the laundry and I remember the cigarette machine above the laundry sink, and you'd put the money above the machine for the Rothmans, you'd put two shillings in and then shoonk...you know, it was a dispensing machine, the Rothman's guy used come around once a week and fill it up again...'

I closed my eyes, picturing the room where I'd recorded mum and the rooms of which she spoke. In the dark, breath-filled world I now inhabited, I felt the weight of Alex's body leave my couch, heard the sound of her feet on the straw mat and the barely audible the return of her body to the other couch.

8. Visual caress

January described her research interests in the style of certain kinds of academic language: she was interested in the relationship between vision, sound, technology and the human body. While she couldn't be certain about the origin, January often used a story that involved the *Terminator* films of the 1990s to make her research more relatable.

As a child, I developed the habit of making sucking noises as a sound effect, said January, to accompany a certain way of looking at things. I imagined this certain way of looking as similar to the android in this film: red-tinted vision, with augmented reality overlays like lists and shapes analysing certain objects and elements in my visual field.

January specified that she didn't *see* in this way of course. Her vision didn't turn red and the world she saw didn't look like the Terminator's vision. But she did feel different when she made the sound and matched it to certain gestures associated with looking, like turning her head.

When she scrutinised her childhood habit in later life, January realised that she had most likely been making multiple sounds: one by sucking air in through the tightly closed gaps between her teeth and lips, and the other by pushing air back out through her tongue and top row of teeth. The first sound accompanied a scanning motion while she looked in a relatively indiscriminate way across her visual field. She made the second sound when focusing in on a particular person or object.

Like a lady in a red cap with a dog, for example, said January. Even though I can't *zoom* with my vision like a camera, the sound effect, and the act of focusing with which it is accompanied, induces a weak, hallucinatory sense of moving closer to the object in view.

I became quite enamoured with January after this brief, personal insight into her research interests. The Head of School had asked me to chat with some of the more senior members in the faculty and help them write about their research for a newsletter. I was a writer, so I could supposedly use my abilities to help academics like January express their research more elegantly in sentences. What's more, I was keen to collect more content for my stories about design, particularly since Beta had mentioned another academic she knew of doing a similar thing and the possibility of arranging a visit for them at the university. A sense of urgency set in regarding the production of my own research: I had to ensure my investigations were significantly enough progressed so that if I did encounter this that it would be recognised collectively my activities were of comparable sophistication and value.

January had one of the most interesting offices in the building and unlike many of her colleagues, she could reliably be found inside it, often tinkering with an object or drawing. Her door, in my experience, was more or less always open. On the occasion of our first meeting, however, her door was closed and locked. Puzzled and a little frustrated, I got a piece of paper from the stationery cupboard and wrote a note to inform her that I'd come by, slipping it under the door. Just as I'd started to wander off, I heard the door open and January called out my name. She explained that she hadn't realised she'd locked the door.

For some reason, said January, after never having done it in the past, I've now started compulsively locking the thing. I've also developed the habit of leaving my phone in the car, she said, although only when I've got it plugged into the audio system. It's as though it vanishes into the console on account of the connection.

January had one of her strange green drinks on her desk and appeared to be doing some design work on a toaster, the form of which resembled a carousel. I'd seen the toaster on her shelf in the past when I walked by her office and she'd described it as the end of an evolutionary line. I couldn't figure out how it worked just by looking. January saw my puzzlement and apologised that she couldn't offer a demonstration at present as she just started pulling the toaster apart.

She gestured towards her bean bag and took a seat herself, swivelling the chair away from me slightly, as though encouraging me to look at an object of mutual interest in the corner of her office.

I re-explained what I'd already said in an email about the purpose of the meeting, asked an initial question about her research, and then January launched into her story about computer vision and *The Terminator*.

Let's look them up, said January, 'zoom' and 'scan'.

We soon discovered that zoom had its origins in aviation, in the vernacular of pilots who used the word to imitate the sense of rapidly moving closer to something: *zoom*.

Ha, said January, and informed me that the verb 'scan' comes from scanning poetry, a process that involves making explicit the rhythm of verse by identifying the stressed and unstressed syllables.

It's an ambivalent word though, said January, as it seems to mean to 'observe closely' and 'look over quickly, to skim'.

I had the sense this might have been a 'discovery' that January performed many times for interested interlocutors like me.

I had come with a story I prepared earlier that I was confident related directly to January's research interests. The story involved someone called Jade, who was in reality my partner.

At some point in her early adult life, Jade started to make a particular sound.

If forced to come up with words to describe its meaning, Jade would, I said, probably use the phrase 'ambient agreement'. The sound also performed a certain emotional function. It gave her the sense that she was inhabiting a space. It communicated her presence, her alertness to the presence of other communicative beings in a space and a willingness to engage with them. To call the sound a hum missed some of its distinctiveness—if it was a hum it was also a sigh. There was something musical about the sound too. A little tune. Jade didn't always make the sound. She thought it had something to do with stress, the stress of adulthood.

January asked whether I knew if the sound accompanied any particular act of looking and I replied, no, it was probably indiscriminate in that regard.

By way of a response to my story, January mentioned another research participant to whom she gave the name Sadie. Sadie's ex-boyfriend, Jet, had alerted her to a soft, high-pitched, slightly nasal groaning sound she made on her outbreath. Sadie had no idea she was making the sound. Jet assumed she made the sound when she was nervous or frustrated.

He started mimicking Sadie, said January, and using the sound when she asked him to do something that he didn't want to do, like watering the pot plants or putting a hook in the wall for a picture. She didn't believe him; didn't believe that she could make such a sound and remain totally unaware of it. Sadie asked Jet to tell her when she was next making the sound. However, perhaps due to obscure machinations of her subconscious, Sadie completely stopped making the sound. Jet suggested she was stopping on purpose to avoid proving him right, but she swore she wasn't intentionally stopping anything, and besides, if it was autonomic anyway, how could she intentionally stop?

But Jet couldn't give up his imitations, continued January, and at some point, rather than being associated with Sadie, the groan became his trademark, a joke—if that's the right word—that he started performing in front of friends. If someone in a group made a decision to go to a restaurant he didn't like, Jet would make the nasal groaning sound and everyone would laugh.

According to January, Sadie and Jet both started to get sick of the sound. Jet had started making the sound all the time, even the most minor effort would be accompanied by the groan, such as when he got off the couch. He vowed that he'd stop making the sound at home but couldn't seem to stop for longer than an hour. He started to curse the moment it escaped his lips, or rather, his nose. Sadie decided that she'd start making the sound too, in the hope that it might reverse the process. For a while Jet got worse. Between the two of them there was more groaning than conversation in the house. But gradually Jet started making the sound less and less. Sadie gradually adjusted the regularity with which she made the sound too.

Soon enough, said January, it completely disappeared from their life and even when they remembered the sound months and years later, it had none of the addictive quality that it previously seemed to possess.

I asked Sadie whether she'd be able to record the sound for me, less so I could hear the sound for myself and more so I could watch her reaction when she played the sound back to herself, with me as an audience. I gave her a recording device and asked Sadie to give the device a name. Annabelle, she said, it looks like an Annabelle.

The next week I attended one of the postgraduate classes January taught on what she called 'second-order perceptual thinking'. I was in part attending to gain a more comprehensive insight into her research. I was also attending because at some point in my previous discussion with January I'd experienced what I can only describe as a deep and binding affinity with her intellect.

I puzzled over how to describe this. For it wasn't exactly the content of January's research that I found inspiring, though it was certainly interesting. It was, rather, *that January was doing this research*. That she was so invested in it. The entity that had commanded my attraction was, in this sense, the expression of an intellectual and emotional investment in an open-ended problem. Neither January nor her research in isolation would, I speculated, have offered the same attraction.

I'd even set to work prototyping different, internally produced sounds of my own to share with January when we next met, perhaps after her class for a coffee. The rigors of my investigative efforts were matched by the importance I placed on the upcoming, hypothetical scenario where January would examine and discipline my ideas with great care and scrutiny, inspiring yet more nuanced and widely applicable discoveries.

I'd named my new sound 'visual caress'.

Coming up with visual caress was harder than I imagined, but once I'd hit on the effect, it seemed to encompass so much of what I did when I looked at things. For example, when I observed a pigeon, about two metres away on the grass, I first thought about zooming and scanning and the sound effects January made to accompany these acts of looking. Then I thought about visually caressing the bird and how this act of looking was similar to, though different from zooming. Both involved looking at something in the distance, but the caress was less to do with focus and more to do with touch, or the feel of the look of a shape: the particular roundness of the pigeon's wing and the more detailed ripple of its grey feathers as they picked up the light. I felt as though I was scooping the bird out of the background, shucking it; it was almost as though I held the form in my hand.

Nice birdy, I said, in the voice of a film character I couldn't remember. *Nishe birdy.* This time pronouncing the 'c' as a 'sh' just to please myself.

I started trying to match different sounds with my visual caress, however, this proved difficult. The first range of sounds I tried were all modelled on what I quickly saw were robotic sounds that belonged to the same set as scanning and zooming mentioned by January. This included rattlings of the tongue against the roof of my mouth and other varieties of sucking: hydraulic sounds, similar to scanning. Then I tried a soft moan, which indicated pleasure too explicitly. It soon became amusing to pair this sound with acts of looking that were incongruously dull, like looking at pole or the painted wooden slats of a bench.

One morning at the beach I continued with my experiments. I found that looking at the skin and form of human bodies was more exciting than looking at other surfaces and shapes. Even though I couldn't always make a sound that matched my mental impression of what I felt the sound should be, I quickly became better at imagining different kinds of sound; half-formed sonic imaginings, matched to particular bodies.. Many of the sounds seemed to emanate directly from the bodies and objects I observed, even though I knew they were simply mental impressions. When a certain body gave me the idea for a sound, I could then abstract this sound from the body of initial inspiration and apply it indiscriminately to the act of looking. For example, I was enjoying watching the glistening skin of a brown body on a towel about fifty metres away and modulating more subtle versions of a groaning sound in the process, then another body moving in my periphery caught my attention, an old man with a hairy back. I became the feeling of his hair scrambling the previous impeccable, glowing skin I'd observed on the other body. The hair seemed to have a sound like white noise. Although I couldn't vocalise this sound, I began using the mental impression of the sound to imagine bodies being scrambled by pores—if that expression makes sense. Even though I didn't see people become more porous as such, with hairs growing out of their bodies, I had an idea of them being this way, which was made more compelling by imagining the scrambling sound in parallel.

Perhaps with January's anecdote in mind, these thoughts and half-thoughts drifted into speculations about the different visual and emotional capacities of a Terminator-type robot. I imagined this robot was able to see the way different humans were sensing their environments at semi-, subconscious and unconscious levels. The robot saw humans as cloud-like forms that continually absorbed, discarded and changed elements of their surrounding niche. This conjectural robot was able to gauge what the human was taking from and putting back out into the environment, anything from air to anxiety. The robot could switch between viewing these emotional, physiological and sensory exchanges between a human and its environment, and seeing what we humans typically see when observing each other.

This sort of parasitic inhabitation of the research interests of another person was not uncommon for me, particularly when I found the researcher charismatic. There was the problem of how much to reveal of my efforts to January: revealing too much of what I'd been up to would be creepy, though just enough might give January an insight into my own intellectual investment, such that she might feel reciprocally, as I had when she shared her stories with me.

January was standing at a lectern when I entered the room. The small class was clustered towards the back, so I made a point of occupying a seat in one of the front rows. January acknowledged me with a glance.

The image on the projection screen at the front of the room showed a diagram of sorts that combined the features of a pie chart with concentric ellipses that telescoped to an inner nucleus containing three, black icons: a house with a pitched roof, the bust of a human and what appeared to be an apartment block. These three icons were clustered tightly together. Most of the screen was taken up by the segments of pie, which shone outwards like rays and cut across the three radial bands of the concentric ellipses.

The colouring of the image reminded me of toothpaste or cleaning products: washed out greens of varying grades to distinguish the different radial bands, with the centre ellipse or nucleus a kind of grey-blue.

On closer inspection, I saw there were three, rather than four, nested ellipses. The fourth, central ellipse, which revealed the aforementioned three icons, was actually a slit or opening in a layer of perfectly uniform white haze that sat above the other three ellipses and blurred out five of the seven pie segments, converting them into background considerations for the purpose of the image, while the middle ellipse and the two exposed segments were foregrounded.

Infographics were scattered within each segment of pie: powerlines of two different kinds, battery icons, solar panels, wind turbines, a seesaw, a clock face, thermometers, a dollar sign, and the cooling towers of a power station. The icons for batteries and powerlines were visible in the foreground segments, showing clear through the haze.

January was hypothesising about the different sets of knowledge an historian of such an image would need to profess. Her dark, slick-down hair, was in this context reminiscent of a military figure, and she spoke in a way that indicated she was invested greatly in the oratory performance she was giving for the small audience.

A question was asked of the room: which elements, if any, stood out most in the image?

No hands were raised. January leaned forward, transferring more of her bodyweight onto her arms and the lectern.

No one?

A student in my periphery looked up from her phone and scrutinised the image for a while through her squinted eyes.

The icons, she said, the little black icons. You see them everywhere.

Good, said January, and she proceeded to give a brief history of a project in the interwar years where a group of researchers sought to develop a universal picture language; that is, a universally understood language using pictures or icons that could be combined in manifold ways to communicate meaning in a manner that surpassed the slow complications and messy diversity of vernacular languages.

According to January, while the researchers were perhaps not entirely successful in achieving their aims, a brief survey of global visual culture gives the impression that our collective efforts to represent widely and quickly understood information has converged, for better or worse, on the aesthetic and form of thought associated with these icons.

January implored her audience to think, for example, of toilet facilities around the world: while minor deviations from the stereotype might be common, there nonetheless seemed to be a collective consensus in large public spaces that best way of designating respective male and female facilities was to use icons represented by abstracted male and female bodies: circular heads, uniform torsos and limbs.

January spoke to the room about how these seemingly perfectly abstracted forms had been refined over many iterations from figurative representations in expressionist works of art, like the woodblock prints of Gerd Arntz. She often wondered about the extent to which the forms of little icons we now take for granted would have been different if the project of a universal picture language had been delayed by a century or so, and if, in this conjectural scenario, designers, linguists and philosophers, instead of turning to expressionism, turned to examples of late-twentieth and early twenty-first century art for their inspiration.

January speculated about the extent to which the icons would differ if the source artworks featured flowing, organic lines using ink or charcoal, like those used by Tracey Emin. Or even subtly different human figures like the shimmering, stooped figures of Antony Gormley's sculptures. To what extent would the abstractions deviate from the present form? Or did the block-like, modular forms of the woodcut medium have an inherent synergy with the moral and pragmatic ambitions of a universal picture language? By contrast, did the spontaneity and distinctiveness of organic, flowing lines remain resolutely unsuited to such a project?

Such easy binaries, continued January, will perhaps appear foolish when our digital technologies come to readily replicate the supposed ipseity of the idealised form of the line, to which I have just given verbal expression.

Now, said January, someone else?

I scrutinised the image, however, all my cognitive activity was taken up with imagining that I was in an unspoken communion with January, where we wandered through the unlikely landscape of the pie chart, as though it were another, alien dimension, utterly inhospitable to human habitation.

It looks like it's been made in PowerPoint, said the same woman who had previously noted the icons.

It does, doesn't it, agreed January. Early twentieth-century office software vernacular. The cave paintings of our epoch.

For the first time I noticed the little soliloquies in square boxes scattered around the outside of the page, one for each segment of pie. I knew nothing about the disembodied being who supposedly spoke the phrases, which began with either: 'I can buy', 'I can generate', 'I can save', 'I can use, or 'I can sell'.

Note, said January, that this image is called *The Customer View* and the customer is at the centre of the page, along with icons denoting their favoured places of living: the free-standing bungalow and the apartment. But you will observe, continued January, that all these icons show things seen from the outside: the house from the outside, the apartment block from the outside, the human from the outside.

The visualisation deals only in exteriors, said January, in external representations of discrete pieces of information. Their icons are impenetrable, pure exterior; its expression in the style of bridges, not nests, burrows or other membranous structures maintained by lifeforms. Despite being the customer view, there is, affirmed January, no notion of psychological space, or what some philosophers might call *dwelling*.

January continued to speculate about how the image appeared to neglect the very dimension of experience it was supposed to represent, whether for purposeful or unintentional reasons.

I would like everyone now, said January, to join with me in a some very basic exercises. The first of these is to imagine that the projection on the screen is blinking. Not a regular blinking like the shutter on a camera, but a varied, unpredictable blinking: now slow, now fast, now frequent, now with long pauses. The view you now see before you, said January, is not in fact a static, omnipresent representation of the world, but the way a particular entity sees, a perspective. In blinking we are imagining ourselves in the position of this so-called entity. Now, hold onto this sense that you are occupying the position of the entity, whose perception configures its reality in such a way. Blink once, slowly, and now when you open your eyes, you are in a park. At first the park will look like a park usually does, with grass of varying grades of green and yellow and brown; with sounds of people at play, yelling phrases and names; with screams of joy and resistance, balls bouncing, bicycle wheels spinning; the general hum of park activity. There is cool air on your face, the distant sound of birds in the bush, the groan of a plane in the sky and the closer groan of a car; there are big people and small people running and walking, putting on shoes, twisting and tilting their bodies for both apparent and obscure reasons; there is food being cooked and unwrapped, cans of drink being cracked open, dogs being gently tugged along on leashes; there is perhaps a mood of boredom or agitated excitement, perhaps a rare passing peace, perhaps the day makes you feel trapped or inspired... all this activity is collected in your perceptual field.

Now, continued January, blink again slowly, and when you open your eyes imagine you see the world as it's viewed by an entity whose perceptual field consists in a style of looking compatible with the image we have just been analysing up on the screen. Divide your park scene into sections using the visual language of lines and geometric forms. Reduce features to uniform colours, and imagine floating partitions of haze blurring out some aspects of the view and highlighting others.

January dimmed the lights and let us inhabit the worlds of our visualisations for a while. I found it impossible to steady my imagination enough so that it remained solely in the mode of the projected image. The previous, richly imagined park would filter back through and I would find myself occupying a composite image, in which perfect sheets of haze drifted between people in animated states of play, and abstract shapes calved up the scenery in dynamic and expressive ways.

January guided the class through one more speculative visualisation activity. She handed out sheets of A4 paper that had nine empty rectangles distributed across the page. I delighted for a moment as I took the page from her hand and a circuit formed between our bodies. She released her grip and moved on to the rest of the class.

The activity required we depict a series of scenes that featured the image projected on the screen. January wanted us to use a technique whereby elements of the image would be used as the basis, or at least have some significant role, for the rest of the scenarios we depicted.

For example, said January, in your first scene you might want to show the image on a computer in a particular office setting where groups of people are pointing to its features or using the image in a particular way. Or you might want to abstract one of the graphic elements from the image and use it to characterise a setting, a prop or even an idea. You might want to use the battery icon on the surface of the frame so that it seems as though we are looking at your scene through the view of an interface that communicates power is an important metric for the consumer. You might even want to show the image halfway through being created, with its maker or makers depicted nearby in postures that indicate acts of decision-making and hesitation.

The empty squares on the sheet of paper made me apprehensive, so I drew a rough half-circle or arch, which was intended to refer to the ellipse in the centre of the projected image. I drew the bust of the human icon inside the circle, the head of which titled slightly one way—as seemed inevitable with the heads of any of human figure I drew.

January continued to give examples and answer questions from the students, who became vocal and anxious now that they were required to commit their thinking to the page.

I had no foreknowledge of the story I was going to depict before I put my pen to paper, however, the elements began to coalesce as I moved across the page. Almost without conscious effort, I studiously filled the first three or so squares with graphic elements derived from the projection. Certain features of the drawing in my first frame became crucial elements of the setting and scenario as it developed. In the second frame I showed the human figure reaching out an arm to touch the dome-like form within which it was enclosed.

In the third frame, I showed the scene experienced from the perspective of the figure. Here I faced my greatest compositional challenge: how could I make explicit that the scene depicted was in fact from the first-person perspective of the figure rather than an omniscient view of the landscape?

After drawing a generic landscape view of the kind people might expect a generic figure to survey, I then shaded the surface of the frame with a few lines to indicate the presence of a reflective, intervening medium between figure and landscape. I realised, after completing the frame, that the first-person perspective would have been even harder to show had the figure not been in a bubble, as the bubble afforded the chance of visually locating the inside-ness of the first person in an external form or medium.

Somewhat half-heartedly, in accordance with the convention of first-person video games, I then drew the arms and hands in the foreground of the image, as though the figure were examining these strange appendages for the first time.

The fourth and fifth frames returned to a third person perspective and showed a crucial moment of change: the figure casting off its transparent bubble to stand exposed in wide-open landscape. The rest of the images showed the figure walking through that landscape on a journey I conceived as I drew: the figure would walk to a different place, identified by electricity infrastructure, such as powerlines and cooling towers, selected from the original image. Here the figure would find a new, upturned bubble for it to occupy, much like a hermit crab.

After I reviewed my story I decided to add some sweat and the expression of a grimace on the face of the figure in the images where it walked without the protective bubble.

Pleased with my efforts, I left the A4 sheet in full view on the foldout table attached to my seat. When January completed her rounds of the class she asked if she could have a look.

Her face became yet more attractive as it showed that she was processing the information I had inscribed on the page.

Do you realise that in a way, she said, you have told the meta-narrative of humanity?

What my story indicated to January, as she soon told the entire class, was that even in conditions where we are given great scope to tell stories of our own choosing we often sub-consciously converge on archetypal tales. As she explained the implications of this to the class and discussed some of the other examples, I wanted to reach up, take my drawing back and append it with new elements, perhaps text boxes, indicating that the story was not so generic and she had misunderstood its complex plot. I found it impossible, however, to imagine what these new additions might be without the sheet of paper on the table before me and a pen in my hand.

After class January joined me for a coffee in the university cafeteria. The hard seats made me uncomfortable to the extent that I periodically tried to sit on my hands for relief. The browning leaves of a plane tree scraped against a thin, horizontal window that showed a uniform strip of grey sky outside.

I had a few recordings on my phone of sounds that I thought matched the visual caress, the best of which was playing cards being shuffled. It's crisper than a purr, I'd imagined myself saying to January, as she listened to the sound. I'm still perfecting my imitation, but it is getting better.

There were other sounds too that I'd tried: sticky tape being unpeeled, rubbing cloth together, the sound of a marble rolling on wood, softly crushing a bag of potato crisps, a gushing tap.

Instead I remained silent and watched January sip from her cappuccino, which, curiously, she described in the singular—*I just love cappuccino*—when I thought it would have been appropriate to use the plural—*I just love cappuccinos*—the missing 's' giving the sense that the drink were manifest to her primarily as one vast substance from which she periodically scooped a portion using a cup, rather than a plurality of continuously emerging cappuccinos contingent on cappuccino drinkers.

Remind me then, said January, why we have arrived here, my memory has been terrible the last few weeks?

Surprised and a little irritated by the newfound glitches that were emerging in what I previously thought was a high-functioning mentor, I started to tell January about how she had told me about her so-called sucking sounds imitating the Terminator and how she matched these with certain acts of looking, scanning and zooming in particular.

The 'visual caress', I said proudly, is my best candidate for a new sound which captures acts of looking that are governed primarily by intimacy and feeling, rather than clarity, identification and analysis.

I then told January how I had, for example, listened to the sound of the water gushing from a tap and continued to hold the memory of this sound in my mind as I walked around a park. I first wondered whether the gushing sound would be appropriate to match with the act of looking I described as 'visual caress' and then I reflected on the extent to which the sound, and my other candidates for sound effects, would work better as pleasing kinds of incongruity, rather than exact matches.

I had observed bodies in my visual field, I continued, while practicing the application of this new act of perception and its hypothetical, attendant sound effects. I imagined different versions of a scrambling sound, a sound that was harsher and more intense than the sound of the waves crashing at the beach. It was a sound I wanted to describe using words that didn't make it seem sinister or violent. I still wanted these acts of looking to be a kind of caress, but as soon as I used the word 'caress'—and indeed, as soon as I reflected on my experiments looking at bodies—the whole enterprise took on an air of creepiness.

I looked at January until I was sure she could see me looking, then, by vibrating my tongue against the roof of my mouth, I made the sound that I thought best imitated the card shuffle.

January smiled, knowingly, opened her mouth slightly, looked me in the eyes and made a similar sound.

Not bad, she said, not bad at all, and she turned away, now looking across the empty café, and performed the same sound again.

Acknowledgements

My place of work in the School of Design at UTS has in significant part afforded me the opportunity to write *Object Coach*. What I've experienced in my daily life there has formed the grist in the mill of my fictionalisation process. In particular I'd like to acknowledge Abby Mellick Lopes, Cameron Tonkinwise and James Novak, who might see shadow impressions of our interactions in some of the stories told here. I'd also like to acknowledge the fellow members of staff who continue to see value in fiction as source of imagination enlargement and cultural insight, and consequently my own value as a member of the school.

I'd also like to thank and acknowledge Steven Connor, an academic mentor whose curious engagement with the mundane has long been a source of inspiration. Steve hosted me at the Centre for Research in the Arts Social Sciences and Humanities at University of Cambridge in 2020, where I wrote some of *Object Coach*. His published work on the relationship between sense and substance was a significant influence for some of the exchanges between the narrator and Destiny in Chapter 9, particularly the brief dialogue about handwashing. I have written about this work elsewhere in my article that bears the perhaps unlikely title, 'Sense, Substance, Fruit: Examining poetic descriptions of how people experience fruits as input for design considerations.' Steve's book *Dream Machines* was also useful for me in the conceptual framing of the design projects that are the focus of *Object Coach*.

Andrea Koch and Chris Gaul and invited me into the research phases of their Soiltech Project, which forms the basis of the narrator's activities in Chapter 5, and thanks to my brother and dad, who are significant presences in the same chapter, my brother in particular.

I'd like to thank my mum and dad who were the most significant ingredients in allowing space for my imagination to fill uninhibited as I grew up. My brother and sister too, as part of that continually giving childhood that persists in my memory and which in some often indirect sense I still write from today.

Love to my new family, particularly Rach, with whom my spirit is firmly entwined and who outruns me with her insight and kindness. And Eamon/ Mr Baby, as a new addition, while this book was coming together.

Of course, Terri-ann White and Upswell too, for seeing the value in this perhaps unusual story and Emily Stewart for her deft and formative editorial work.

Lastly, I'd like to acknowledge the Gadigal, Wiradjuri, and the Dharawal people, on whose ancestral lands this book for the most part came together. I'd like to pay my respect to the elders past and present and to acknowledge that Australia is unceded land.

About Upswell

Upswell Publishing was established in
2021 by Terri-ann White as a not-for-profit
press. A perceived gap in the market for
distinctive literary works in fiction, poetry
and narrative non-fiction was the motivation.
In her years as a bookseller, writer and then
publisher, Terri-ann has maintained a watch
on literary books and the way they insinuate
themselves into a cultural space and are
then located within our literary and cultural
inheritance. She is interested in making books
to last: books with the potential to still be
noticed, and noted, after decades and thus
be ripe to influence new literary histories.

About this typeface

Book designer Becky Chilcott chose
Foundry Origin not only as a strong,
carefully considered, and dependable
typeface, but also to honour her late
friend and mentor, type designer Freda
Sack, who oversaw the project. Designed
by Freda's long-standing colleague,
Stuart de Rozario, much like Upswell
Publishing, Foundry Origin was created
out of the desire to say something new.